'You have need
and admit you
me, some warn
contact, some bloody body-
bonding!'

She swung back, her eyes wide with defiance.
'But that isn't enough for you, is it, Rupert?
You want the whole package, my body! Well,
you'll just have to go stuff that chicken because
that's the nearest you'll get to any body-
bonding while we share this house!'

Dear Reader

The arrival of the Mills & Boon Mothers' Day Pack
means that Spring is just around the corner . . . so why
not indulge in a little romantic Spring Fever, as you
enjoy the four books specially chosen for you?
Whether you received this Pack as a gift, or bought it
for yourself, these stories will help you celebrate this
very special time of year. So relax, put your feet up and
allow our authors to entertain you!

The Editor

AN IMPERFECT AFFAIR

BY

NATALIE FOX

MILLS & BOON LIMITED
ETON HOUSE   18-24 PARADISE ROAD
RICHMOND   SURREY   TW9 1SR

*First published in Great Britain 1992
by Mills & Boon Limited*

© Natalie Fox 1992

*Australian copyright 1992
Philippine copyright 1993
This edition 1993*

ISBN 0 263 77806 1

*Set in Times Roman 11 on 12 pt.
91-9302-48869 C*

Made and printed in Great Britain

CHAPTER ONE

'You!'

The very male figure seated at a desk by the bedroom window of the old Spanish mill house had turned as Verity opened the door. Their mutual shock at the sight of each other, the stunned disbelief in both their eyes, had erupted with that simultaneous 'You'.

Shocked, Verity gripped the iron handle of the door till her fingers went white, but it was red that flamed through her in a fiery second of realisation. This wasn't some freak coincidence. This had been *arranged*!

Her violet eyes flashed round the bedroom and in a split second took everything in. Rupert Scott was living here, and working too. A lap-top computer was on the desk and papers were strewn everywhere; on the floor, on the bed.

They had met twice before, under awkward and embarrassing circumstances, and now this. Verity couldn't believe the man was here in this remote Andalucian mill house. El Molino, the house her cousin, Stuart, had arranged for her to work in for a month. She'd kill Stuart for this when she got back to England, slowly and painfully.

Rupert Scott found his voice before Verity could summon hers. A deep voice she remembered well — it had haunted her enough times since first they had met.

5

'What the hell are you doing here?' he growled.

Nothing had changed. His tone was as derisive as ever. He was as good-looking as ever too, though she'd never seen him like this before, so very laid-back in his mode of dress.

Verity's voice came back in a spluttering rush with a not very original exclamation. 'I could ask you the same question!'

She had a ghastly feeling that he probably thought this was her idea, as he probably thought their other meetings had been engineered by her. After all, Rupert Scott could be considered quite a catch, in a monetary sense; his personality wasn't such a snip. The man was cool, aloof, and wretchedly moody. But at least they had one thing in common: neither liked being matchmade by her cousin. Oh, yes, if Stuart was to step into the room now she would happily garrotte him for this, and she had a feeling Rupert Scott would readily assist her.

'This is beginning to get boring,' Rupert grated through tight lips. 'First the dinner party your cousin arranged for us, then that "accidental" meeting in a Knightsbridge restaurant, and now this. Can't you and your persistent cousin take a hint?'

Verity burned with embarrassment. She didn't want to be reminded about that awful match-making dinner party and that excruciating incident in the restaurant when Stuart had hovered over Rupert as he had dined alone, clutching her to his side as if she were a sacrificial offering. Of course he had asked them to join him—what else could he have done?—but he had made it quite obvious that he wasn't impressed with Stuart Bolton's cousin, who was being so determinedly pressed on him at every opportunity.

'Why are *you* here?' she blurted to cover her shock and embarrassment.

The 'arranged' theory swelled by the second. Stuart and her editor, Alan Sargeant, had set this up for her. A month in a converted mill house in Andalucia. Not a holiday, not in January, for she was here to work, but a change of scene after a bout of flu that had laid her out over Christmas and, as Alan had reiterated, she'd had a rough time after her boyfriend's death and needed some space and time on her own. This wasn't on her own, though. Rupert Scott was here and Verity was inflamed.

'To work; what does it look like?' was his sharp retort, which sliced into her fury.

'Yes, I can see that! I'm not blind!' she huffed impatiently. 'But why here of all places? Andalucia, in a remote mill house, miles from anywhere. Why did you have to pick this place?'

'Because it's quiet and peaceful—at least, it *was*.' His barbed sarcasm left no doubt he thought her a disruptive nuisance, just as he had at that dinner party and the restaurant. The man didn't like her and she didn't like him, and finding each other in the same house was incredibly awful.

'Is this your house?' she blurted.

'Is it yours?' he countered coldly.

'Well, this is getting us a long way, isn't it?' she spiked back. 'At least we've established this place belongs to someone else.'

'A friend of your cousin's, I was led to believe,' he drawled and stood up as he did so. Verity thought he was going to come towards her and bodily throw her out, but he folded his arms across his chest and leaned back on the desk. 'So perhaps you'd better explain your presence here,' he added.

'I'm here to work!' Verity exploded and then suddenly the fizz went out of her as sheer embarrassment swamped her once again. This must look dreadful to him. She actually felt more sorry for him than herself. She dragged a fretful hand through her pale blonde hair. 'Look, this is ridiculous,' she said levelly. 'Stuart arranged for me to come here for a break——'

'Did he, now?' he interrupted disbelievingly. 'Am I supposed to swallow that?' Before she could answer he went on, 'I don't, not for a minute. I know why you're here and so do you, so shall we stop pussyfooting?'

Verity's eyes widened and her mouth opened and shut as if she'd forgotten how to work it.

He gave her a grim smile. 'And don't come on as if you haven't a clue what I'm getting at. You're here to work your sexy charms on me. You're here to seduce me, aren't you?' Rupert Scott accused drily, his eyes glinting with what Verity could only assume to be disgust.

She matched his outrage and worked her mouth into a cry of horror. 'What?' The very thought, the very idea... She realised that her hand was still fused to the door handle and was aching badly. She let it go and pumped her fist at her side to get the blood flowing again.

Slowly, almost wearily, as if boredom had suddenly hit him, he said, 'Look, dear, you're a sweet kid but absolutely not my type...'

'Don't sweet kid or dear me!' Verity bit back. 'You're light years from my type too, I assure you. I thought you would have got the message on our previous meetings. As for seducing you, heaven forbid! Some hyper-imagination you have!'

His grey eyes darkened threateningly. 'Look, I don't believe for a minute this meeting is pure coincidence. I know exactly why you're here but you can forget it. No sale!'

No sale! Verity gaped at him, gazing at his shabby black tracksuit. He had a long red scarf draped several times round his throat for warmth, and heavy army-type boots on his feet. At Stuart's dinner party he'd been dressed formally in a black evening suit and he'd looked strikingly handsome; not handsome enough to impress her, though, and now he didn't impress her either, just made her so flaming mad that she wanted to bite his knees. His eyes were too grey, his mouth too mean, his hair too damned black and long, and 'no sale' went for her too.

She pushed her long golden hair from her face and steeled herself. 'I'm here to work,' she told him defiantly, 'not to mess with you. My cousin arranged for me to stay here——'

'And me too,' he interrupted icily. 'And, though I admire your cousin's ambition, I can't say I'm enamoured by his methods. I thought I made it quite obvious that night and at the restaurant that I take exception to being manipulated. I don't do blind dates and I don't do business in bed. Tell your cousin that when you get back.'

'Business in bed?' Verity echoed with horror. She dredged her memory pool to recall what he did for a living. And it was some living she remembered. Airline company, state-of-the-art recording studio, film company, so what had all that to do with bed?

His mean mouth broke into a cynical smile. 'Don't look so innocent, treasure. You know exactly what I'm getting at.'

Verity actually stepped further into the room, though her senses told her she ought to be thinking of getting out, back down that twisty mountain road to the coast, back to the airport and home to give her cousin a stripping-down for this. But she was curious, madly curious to know what all this was about. 'I wouldn't look so innocent if I had a clue what you were getting at.'

'Wouldn't you? Blondes have always struck me as being a contradiction of the old adage, dumb.'

Folding her arms across her scarlet sweat-shirt, Verity told him haughtily, 'I'm certainly not dumb but at the moment you are talking in riddles I find difficult to comprehend. If that's dumb, I'm it! So could you repeat what you just said and enlarge on it? I would like to know what my cousin and I are being accused of.'

'Frankly I don't think there's a name for it, and frankly I don't believe you don't know why this ridiculous charade has been set up.'

And it was a set-up, Verity inwardly agreed, a matchmaking set-up, though she failed to understand why this man needed someone to organise his love-life—he looked very capable of doing that for

himself. She didn't fancy him but she could imagine other women tripping over their hormones to
get to him. He had a certain bile-churning attraction—to sows!

'I want more than that!' she told him bitterly. 'I
want a full explanation and a damned apology for
thinking I'm here to bed you.'

He actually smiled. 'An apology for the truth you
won't get from me, and if there's any explaining to
do there's a phone in the village. Call your cousin
on the way back to the airport and tell him his
scheme won't work. I can't be bought with sexual
favours.'

He sat down and swung back to his work and
started tapping away at his computer. Verity's blood
started to overheat. Sexual favours! The man was
crazy *and* he expected her to go—and now!

'You expect me to go? Just as if I lived round
the corner?' She took a deep defiant breath when
he made no attempt to answer. He owed her an
explanation and an apology and she was going to
get both before she left.

'I've endured a delay at Heathrow Airport, a two-
and-a-half-hour flight with a plastic lunch and an
hour and a half of cross-country rallying to get
here,' she rattled on crossly. 'I arrive here expecting the same peace and quiet you did, and what
do I find when I'm exploring the rooms? A
nightmare in the form of you. I'm tired, thirsty and
hungry and I'm damned well going to satisfy my
needs before *you* dictate to me what I should do!
So stick that up your jumper, Mr Rupert Un-
Bearable, and incubate it!'

She stormed from the room and slammed the door after her and tore down the stone stairs to the kitchen. When she got there, breathless with fury and exertion, she slumped into a kitchen chair and held her head in her hands.

This was *awful*! So awful that she just didn't know what to do. She looked up, out of the window. The sun had gone, dipping down over some distant hill. It was suddenly colder than ever in this cavernous house, and exhaustion claimed her. She would have to drive down that fearful, twisty, narrow road back to the airport in the dark. Her return flight was a month from now and she'd have to mess around trying to get another flight back, struggling with her luggage, all alone ... She covered her face and very nearly burst into tears.

She felt a hand on her shoulder. 'Beryl, I'm——'

'The name's Verity, Verity Brooks!' she snapped, swatting at his hand as if it were a disease-carrying mosquito. 'Get your hands off me!' Damn him! He hadn't even remembered her name!

She felt the warmth recede, heard him moving across the room to the sink.

'I'm sorry, Verity. It's a bit unfair of me to expect you to go immediately. The morning will do.'

'Oh, how very considerate of you!' she blazed sarcastically. 'Why don't *you* go? I've as much right here as you have!' She wasn't going to go without a fight—hell! She wasn't going to go at *all*!

He didn't answer till he'd filled a kettle and plugged it in. 'Squatters' rights, I'm afraid. I've been here a week already and have no intention of packing up and getting out to please the whims of

you. I'm in the middle of an important project——'

'I don't care if you're in the middle of a mid-life
crisis!'

'Too young. Now will you stop hissing at me like
a she-cat and listen to some good down-to-earth
reasoning?'

Her eyes flashed warningly at him when she
realised he was quite angry now. Well, she was mad
too, and she had more reason to be than him!

'Only if it's constructive,' she iced back. 'This
situation is quite intolerable and you are making it
worse. I arrived here in all innocence, not knowing
you were here, but you seem to think it's some sort
of scheme to get us together. I promise you, I
wouldn't have come if I'd thought you'd be here.
You talk of seduction and business in bed and I
don't know what the blazes is going on!'

'I don't know you well enough to believe you're
not in on this,' he insisted darkly. 'So perhaps you'd
better start by explaining exactly why you *think* you
are here.'

He held her warring eyes with those of steely fire
and Verity felt the heat scorch through her. Now
she knew what it felt like to be interrogated. So this
was the famed Spanish Inquisition, was it?

'Why I *think* I'm here?' she flamed. 'I know
exactly why I'm here...to work. Nothing more
sinister than that, whatever your corrupted mind
wishes to deceive you with!'

She didn't know if he believed her or not; he
simply asked if she wanted tea or coffee.

Surprised, she uttered, 'Tea, please, decaf-
feinated if there is any.' She ignored his intake of

resigned breath at that. 'You don't believe me; you don't believe I'm here to work, do you?'

'I'm getting a little tired of this game,' he told her brittly as he measured tea into a metal teapot. 'Were you or were you not despatched here to lower my resistance with a seduction attempt?'

Verity laughed, incredulously. 'Don't take this as a compliment but you hardly appear to be an easy push-over, and I'm certainly no *femme fatale*.'

He smiled, and it was the first indication that he believed her, though Verity wished it wasn't because of that *femme fatale* remark. Blonde and innocent she might look, but she was streetwise enough to cope with his brash arrogance.

'So what were your intended tactics if they weren't to bed me into compliance?'

Compliance with what, for heaven's sake?' she croaked back in shocked disbelief. This conversation was getting ridiculous and her patience was running dry.

Her strangled reply had him looking at her with sudden doubt, as if he just might be beginning to believe her. 'Have you any idea what I'm talking about?' he murmured.

'None whatsoever, but no doubt some time this century you'll get around to speaking without a forked tongue.'

She watched and waited while he made the tea, and she remembered the sour milk she'd found in the fridge while she was exploring on her arrival.

'No milk,' she told him quickly.

She should have known then that the old mill was already occupied. There were enough signs lying around: the dirty dishes in the sink, keys on the kitchen table, the back door unlocked. She had stepped into the house, naïvely thinking that the maid who came with the property was here preparing for her stay. No maid, just his arrogant self. Goldilocks, discovering the grumpy grizzly bear.

He poured two cups of black tea and brought them to the table, setting one down in front of her and one across from her. He sat and faced her, leaned back and gazed directly into her eyes.

'Tell me, Verity Brooks, tell me why you are here?'

God, how she hated his supercilious tone and the penetrating way he looked at her. 'I've already told you! I'm here to work.'

'What work? Scrubbing floors, plumbing——'

'Don't try getting funny with me,' she cut in quickly. 'There's nothing funny about this situation whatsoever.'

She had the power to annoy him. She felt satisfaction at that as his eyes glowered and his facial muscles pulsed. 'I wasn't trying to be funny, and will you quit fancy-footing around every question I drop in your lap? Let's resolve this before I lose my patience.'

Verity leaned forward. 'Well, I have a patience too and at the moment it's full of holes. If you just shut up for five minutes and let me have my say neither of us needs lose our cool.'

He didn't like that, being spoken to as if he were five. So what? Oh, boy, did he irritate her. So badly that her skin fizzed with it. She analysed that irritation and found that it stemmed from his forgetting her name. She hadn't forgotten his, or anything about him, but nightmares had that effect on her!

'Well?' he prompted when she added nothing.

She leaned back in her chair and tried to relax. Hard when a nightmare faced you across the table. So, if he hadn't remembered her name she doubted he'd remembered her occupation. 'I'm features editor of a health and beauty magazine. *Looks Healthy*,' she told him, wondering if she was jogging any memory cells. 'I had the flu over Christmas and I'd just returned to work and my editor, Alan——'

'Alan Sargeant?' he exclaimed, and his brow furrowed threateningly.

'Yes...yes,' Verity murmured in puzzlement. 'You know him?' If he did he didn't look too happy about it.

Rupert nodded as if something was suddenly dawning on him, 'Go on.'

'Alan thought I needed a break,' Verity went on, masking off the apprehension that was suddenly misting her thoughts. Was Alan involved in this supposed conspiracy too? 'We'd planned a book, a spin-off from the magazine I work for. We've done them before. This one's a book for brides-to-be, how to get fit for the big day. Diets and exercise regimes, that sort of thing. Most of the groundwork has been done by one of the other editors and now it just needs putting together, and Alan thought it a good idea to pack me off here for a month to do it.' She wasn't going to tell him about Mike's death; that was no concern of his.

'And?'

'And what?'

'And that's it?'

Verity wrapped her hands round her cup to warm her fingers. She was getting colder by the minute. Stuart had warned her that it might be chilly in the hills, but she hadn't been prepared for this cavernous house with its solid stone walls, seemingly to be hewn out of the very rock it was built against.

'Yes, that's it,' she murmured, her jaw aching from fighting to stop her teeth from chattering. 'Nothing more, nothing less.'

'What a very considerate boss you have. A month in Spain, all expenses paid, no doubt. Sounds too good to be true, and what has your cousin to do with this?'

The edge to his voice added to her apprehension. 'A . . . a friend of his owns this place and it was vacant——'

'But it wasn't,' he cut in. 'I'm here and Stuart knew that—it was he who offered me the place. What connection has he with your boss, Alan Sargeant?'

'Questions, questions,' she couldn't help retorting. 'In spite of the dinner party and the restaurant and the fact that Stuart loaned you this place, you really don't know him very well at all, do you?'

'And after this little mystery I don't think I want to. Now are you going to tell me the connection or not?'

'They met at university and have been close friends ever since; in fact, they're related too. Stuart's wife, Angie, is Alan's sister, so they're brothers-in-law,' Verity efficiently informed him, though what difference it would make to this situation she couldn't imagine.

'Aha, the plot thickens!' Rupert gave a cynical smile and lifted his cup to his mouth.

'What plot?' Verity husked. She didn't know it, but her eyes had widened innocently.

'Is that an act?'

'What?'

'That innocent look in your eyes.'

Verity slammed her cup down on the table. 'A Thespian I'm not, impatient I am. Will you kindly tell me what is going through your mind?'

'Don't you think this all rather a little odd?' he suggested darkly. 'First the dinner party to bring us together, then that contrived meeting in the restaurant, and now this.'

Verity lowered her lashes. At the time she had been mad with Stuart for trying to pair her off with this man. But later she had forgiven him. She understood that he'd done it out of love and concern for her. She had lost Mike but she didn't want another man in her life so soon after their rocky relationship had ended so tragically. She wanted time and space to pick up the pieces and try to forget and had thought she had got her point through to her cousin. Apparently not. Stuart was convinced that she needed a new man in her life and it was this one sitting across from her. Rupert Scott.

'I like it even less than you,' she husked and then bravely raised her eyes to his. 'Listen. I've no interest in you whatsoever,' she told him earnestly. 'I'm sure Stuart's intentions were . . . were . . .'

'Don't say honourable or thoughtful or kind,' he warned sardonically, his eyes sheet-metal grey and hard. 'I loathe these sort of manipulative tactics and I dread to think what nonsense they've stuffed your pretty little head with——'

'Will you stop this and tell me what is going on?' she pleaded.

His lips tightened and she thought she would never prise the truth from them. Why were they both here? It certainly wasn't a coincidence. It had been plotted and planned, she was convinced of that now, but why was he so reluctant to tell her the truth?

He stood up suddenly and gathered up the dirty cups. If she knew him better she might be led to believe that he didn't want to face her. He spoke at last, almost kindly but verging on patronisingly.

'I believe you now. You really don't know what is going on, do you?'

Verity could only shake her head.

'Perhaps your cousin is cleverer than I thought, or maybe subtler is a more accurate description.'

'I still don't know what you are getting at,' Verity murmured.

'Why do you think we are both here?'

Verity swept her hair from her face and shifted uncomfortably in her seat. 'I . . . I presume it was another of Stuart's matchmaking attempts.'

He laughed and shook his head. 'I can find my own women when I want them, and you're a pretty snappy-looking girl yourself—I shouldn't think you have any problems picking up a man. No, treasure, this is far more devious than it appears.'

'And you know precisely how devious, don't you?' Her heart was beginning to thud dangerously. It was a ridiculous situation. The dinner party was excusable on reflection, but not the restaurant and this third attempt? Teaming the two of them in an isolated mill house in Andalucia was...was determined, to say the least. 'Stuart and Alan are in this together, aren't they?' she breathed heavily.

'I'm afraid so,' Rupert grated, drawing a hand through his thick black hair. 'At first I thought you were a part of the scheme, but I don't think you're that good a liar.' His eyes narrowed at her sharp intake of breath, but he didn't apologise. 'It doesn't change anything. We are here together and what they expected to happen isn't difficult to imagine. But bedding you won't change my mind.'

Bedding? Verity shook her head, not believing what she was hearing. An affair with this man? Was that what her two so-called friends wanted and expected? But for what, she couldn't imagine. No, the idea was impossible. The chill inside her froze to the depths of her soul. They were chalk and cheese, as compatible as fire and water, even less likely of making a perfect match than her and Mike. And Mike was dead, but this man was very much alive, and if she stayed...

She suppressed a shudder of dread and opened her mouth to speak, and when the words came out they were very determined and strong.

'I think you'd better tell me everything you suspect,' she directed at him coolly, 'but before you do let's get one thing straight. You're right. I'm not a part of this and I'm not a liar. If there is a plot I know nothing about it. I came here in innocence and I plan to leave here in innocence too. I think you know what I mean.'

His lips tightened and his smoky grey eyes held hers. 'I know exactly what you mean,' he smoothed silkily.

Suddenly he stepped towards her and she flinched as he lifted a tendril of her long, silky fair hair from her shoulder. Surprised and confused, Verity closed her eyes for an instant as he rolled the pale golden tendril between his fingers and thumb as if testing its quality and strength, and when she opened her eyes and looked up at him with wide-eyed innocence he gave her a lazy smile that tightened her stomach muscles into a knot of apprehension.

Very quietly, very suggestively, he husked, 'Innocence, huh? I wonder just how innocent you are, Verity Brooks. You look it, you breathe it, but I wonder.'

'Well, wonder no longer and take my word for it, Rupert Scott,' she breathed defiantly. 'I don't do business in bed either.'

'Business might not come into it,' he told her, his voice so softly timbred that she was more afraid than ever. 'Let's not make promises we can't keep because that would be an added complication. Instead, let's both keep our options open on that innocence statement of yours, shall we?'

She didn't answer; she *couldn't* answer. That apprehension knotted inside her balled to something bigger and far more worrying. All the same, she held his grey eyes as defiantly and as determinedly as he held hers.

She wondered just how far he would push her with shrouded threats like that, for at this moment he was a far cry from that aloof, sophisticated man who had shown so little interest in her in the company of others. But they weren't in the company of others now, they were isolated together in so-called romantic Andalucia, where you could reach out and kiss the moon and clasp a handful of stars to your heart. And Rupert Scott wasn't half so daunting here, and yet he was, and suddenly he seemed very interested indeed in her and she wondered if she hated him as much as she had hyped herself up to.

That was a very perturbing conclusion to come to, one that warranted more tentative thought— later.

CHAPTER TWO

'So...so what's going on here?' Verity asked when Rupert had sat down again. She nervously smoothed her hand over her hair where he had touched it. It was soft and silky and she wondered what had gone through his mind when he had felt it, though, given time, it wouldn't have taken much guessing. It had been an intimate gesture and unexpected, and she wasn't at all sure about the feeling that it had pulsed in her veins. She was beginning to feel a bit soft in the head and dangerously vulnerable.

'Your cousin runs an advertising agency and Alan Sargeant is an ambitious editor, and——'

'And what's that got to do with us?' she interrupted.

'Let me finish and you'll find out.'

Verity clutched her numb fingers in her lap. 'I'm sorry. Carry on.'

'I have various companies that put out a lot of advertising. In a year I spend on promotion what some companies pay their staff. At the moment I'm considering adding a cable-television franchise to my corporation, increasing my Atlantic fleet of aircraft, restructuring the film company and expanding the recording outfit.'

Verity nearly laughed out loud at that verbal scrolling of his business interests. There he was, sitting across from her, looking like a latent hippie in his tracksuit and boots and hardly the pecunious man he had appeared at the dinner party. She bet he was warm, though. She shivered and concentrated her thoughts on what he was getting at.

'And Stuart is pitching for all your advertising,' she suggested.

Rupert nodded. 'He's too small, though. I've already told him that. We met last year and I like and admire him, but I can't use him. The agency I use is the biggest in Europe.'

'Spencers?'

He frowned. 'So you *do* know more about this than you're letting on.'

She shook her head. 'No, I don't, but I'm in the publishing business and know they're the biggest and the best.' Her eyes widened painfully as she looked at him. 'You thought that I was here to seduce you for your advertising account?' Her stomach constricted at the thought.

'I'm afraid so.'

Verity's eyes narrowed in disbelief. She was beginning to feel very bitter about this, with Stuart for exposing her to such humiliation and Rupert Scott for believing she was capable of such a despicable action.

'If I were the Delilah you thought I was when I arrived I'd be in on this—and I'm not.' She glared at him. 'You do believe me, don't you?'

He nodded his very dark head. 'I've already told you that I do. If I didn't you wouldn't be sitting there shivering now, you'd be well on your way back to the airport with a flea in your ear.' He stood up. 'I'll do something about warming this place up.'

Verity stood up with him, her legs wobbling a bit with fatigue. 'But we haven't finished yet.'

She rubbed her forehead fretfully. It wasn't as simple as that. There was more, much more. So she wasn't here to seduce him but she was here nevertheless, and so was he, and Stuart and Alan had arranged it all.

'You suggested that Stuart put me up to this, but you were wrong. I knew nothing about it and, besides . . . besides, he wouldn't do that sort of thing.' Hurt suddenly filled her. 'Stuart is my cousin; he cares about me. He wouldn't use me this way.'

He held her eyes steadily. 'Who knows what slimy depths a man will sink to if his back's against the wall?'

'And what exactly do you mean by that?' Verity asked fiercely. She loved her cousin and no one would put him down behind his back, least of all *this* man.

Rupert let out a disgruntled sigh. 'Look, Verity, I'm not into causing family rifts. If you want answers, go home and ferret them out of your cousin.' He turned away to go through to the vaulted sitting-room, and Verity caught at his arm as he went past her.

'No, you don't,' she exploded. 'You started all this, so you finish it. You've made sickening accusations since I've arrived, and for all I know they're a pack of wicked lies.'

He prised her white fingers from the sleeve of his tracksuit and his metallic grey eyes penetrated hers deeply. 'I'm not a liar, Verity, and I have precious little time to waste on arguing the toss with you. Tell me something: do you love your cousin?'

'Of course I do!' she retorted indignantly. 'We're more like brother and sister than cousins. What has that got to do with all this?'

'Everything,' he replied tightly. 'Families are re-nowned for closing ranks to outsiders in times of trouble and anxiety. I'm that outsider at the moment and you wouldn't believe a word said against Stuart, so this conversation is going pre-cisely nowhere. I came here to work, not to get in-volved with family problems.'

Verity followed him through to the sitting-room and stood behind him as he knelt to rake the dead ashes in the huge grate.

'That's not fair to me,' she told the back of his head. 'What do you mean by trouble and anxiety? You seem to know more about my cousin's business affairs than I do at the moment. I came here in all innocence to work too. This is equally if not more unpleasant for me. You've hinted at——'

'At too much already,' he grated over his shoulder as he made a pile of kindling in the grate.

'And you're not prepared to tell me more?'

He swivelled on his haunches to look up at her. 'Look, Verity, this has nothing to do with me. I can't be expected to take on family hassles. I'm a busy man——'

'Oh, to hell with you!' Verity cried in frus-tration, and swung away and headed back to the kitchen.

'Where are you going?' he called after her.

'Home, of course. Back to England. I'm not staying to have obscure accusations made of my family. You're right, we close ranks to outsiders.' She stopped and glared across the room at him. 'I sincerely hope we don't ever meet again. If we do, it will be my pleasure to sock you in the jaw for your damned arrogance!' She swung round and carried on.

'Haven't you forgotten something?' he called after her.

She stopped once again. 'Yes, of course, my manners. Thanks for the tea!'

'I meant your luggage,' he sighed irritably.

'I didn't bring it in. I must have had a premonition of impending doom!' she bit back icily, and strode purposefully on.

She wrenched open the kitchen door and flew out into fresh air. Cold fresh air and it was dark too, and the bastard wasn't even going to try to stop her!

She hurried down the steps to the pink driveway. The thought of finding her way back down to the coast with just the lights of her car to guide her was terrifying. Some gentleman he was! He might have suggested she stay the night at least. She recalled that he had and then things had got a bit sticky... Damn him and damn her silly pride. If she weren't so stubborn she could have got a good night's sleep before leaving. But her stubbornness was nothing to his. He should have told her what was going on. But in one way he was right—she probably wouldn't have believed him. He could have tried, though, instead of taking that damned secretive attitude.

Lights suddenly blazed across the driveway. That was something at least. He'd put the outside lights on so that she could see to load the car up. When she'd arrived in her hired car from the airport she had unloaded everything on to the drive, and then she had run up the steps to the terrace where Stuart had told her the key would be under a flowerpot. She had found no key and had wandered round to the side of the house and found the back door open, and the rest had been a nightmare discovery: Rupert Scott, here in this house and as awful as ever.

The groceries she'd bought on the coast had toppled and were strewn across the driveway. She squatted down to gather them together when a hand hauled her up.

'Get back inside the house. I'll see to this.'

Her first reaction was to lash out at him for touching her again, but he seemed to know how she felt and his grip tightened on her arm.

'Don't argue, Verity. I'm not the heartless monster you think I am. Get back up to the house and find a bedroom and bathroom—there are enough of them—and we'll talk about this later.'

She didn't argue. Not one word of protest passed her lips. Wearily she left him to it, climbing back up the stone steps and thanking God that he had a heart after all. She'd never have made that drive back to the airport in the dark, and she was too exhausted to even argue with that awful man.

The massive studded front door was open now and she stepped directly into that cavernous main room which gave her the shivers. Stone steps rose to a gallery above the room and then more steps to the bedrooms. Verity took them wearily, forking left on a stone landing. His room was right. She wanted to be as far away from him as possible. She picked the smallest of the two bedrooms available, the one with twin beds and its own small bathroom opening off from it. She sat on her hands on one of the beds and waited for him to bring her case up. Her thoughts went to Stuart and Alan. What on earth were they up to? She knew her cousin wanted to expand his agency, but surely not at the price of her honour? No, Rupert Scott was very wrong.

'Thank you,' she murmured as Rupert put her case down at the foot of the bed. He placed her computer carefully next to it.

'Have you switched on the water heater?' he asked and went to the bathroom to check if she had.

'No. I didn't know there was one.' She stood up and followed him to the small bathroom and stood in the doorway.

He flicked a switch behind the door. 'It will take a while to heat up, so if you're desperate for a bath or shower you're welcome to use my bathroom.'

His bedroom had been none too tidy and she could anticipate the disarray in his bathroom, and declined the offer abruptly. 'I'll wait, thanks.'

'Suit yourself,' he muttered equally shortly, and brushed past her to step back into the bedroom.

Verity stiffened at the closeness of his body as he moved past her. He'd felt warm and smelled of soap and maleness. She couldn't believe she'd noticed that.

He turned at the door. 'I'll light the fire downstairs—you look perished. You must be hungry too. I can't promise a feast; I don't cook, but I'll rustle something up for us.'

'Thanks,' she murmured and then wondered what she was thanking him for. He *owed* her.

Verity unpacked only what she'd need for the night after he'd gone: her toiletries and nightdress and a change of clothes. She slid into the warmest clothes she had, ribbed leggings and a baggy chenille sweater in a deep mulberry shade. She was glad she'd heeded Stuart's warning that the nights could be cold in the foothills and packed warm things. She slid her feet back into her trainers, flicked a comb through her straight, glossy hair and rubbed at a trace of smudged mascara under her eyes. Except it wasn't mascara but shadows of weariness, and she wasn't surprised. What a day! She longed for a bath and bed, but she longed for food more.

She ran downstairs. A fire was blazing in the grate and as yet it hadn't taken the chill off the huge room; nevertheless, it was a welcome sight. She stopped to warm her hands on it and then went through to the kitchen, hoping that Rupert Scott wasn't trying to give the kiss of life to that limp salad she'd seen in the fridge earlier. It was on the table when she walked in.

'I hope we're not eating that,' she said disdainfully.

'No, I was about to throw it out, but now you're here you can.' He was bent over a pan of soup on the hob, stirring it intently.

Verity looked round the room for a pedal bin but only found a brimming plastic carrier-bag in the corner by the larder.

'How often does the maid come in?'

'Never,' he told her. 'I paid her off when I arrived.'

'That accounts for the state the place is in,' she mumbled as she shook the salad out into the carrier-bag and added the dirty bowl to the pile in the sink.

'You could do that washing-up while you're there,' he suggested.

'I'll do nothing of the sort,' she retorted. 'You shouldn't have got rid of the maid. Why did you? You're obviously not house-trained.' She thought she saw a flicker of a smile at the corner of his mouth.

'I came here for solitude, not female chatter.'

'So what happens about the chores?'

'Well, you're here now, so it doesn't present a problem.'

'I'm not clearing up after you!'

'But I'm making supper for both of us. The least you can do is help,' he reasoned, quite pleasantly.

She could have argued that clearing up his dirty crocks—probably a week's worth, by the look of the pile—was hardly a fair exchange for a measly tin of soup, but she went to it none the less.

'I packed your groceries away for you.'

'You can have them. I can't take them with me when I go.'

'So you're going, are you?'

She was so fascinated at the sight of him hacking at a loaf of bread that she took a while to answer. She'd never seen anything quite like it. The slices were wedge-shaped, and she supposed he had hordes of minions to look after him at home.

'First thing in the morning, that's if you don't mind me staying the night.' She turned back to the sink and scrubbed at a cereal bowl and wondered what she would say to Alan when she got back so soon—which reminded her.

'What interest would Alan have in sending me here?' she asked him, aware that that was almost an admittance that there had been a conspiracy.

'I'm thinking of starting a few magazines of my own. In-flight magazines, music and film publications. Sargeant has already approached me for editorship.'

'Hmm, I'm not unduly surprised at that,' she murmured. 'Alan always has some new scheme simmering away in his mind.' Yes, he was ambitious, but that had nothing to do with her. She wouldn't be able to sway Rupert Scott his way even if she succeeded in seducing him. Though she hardly knew the man, she believed him when he said he didn't do business in bed—he didn't need to! Furiously she wrung the cloth out and viciously wiped down the tiled work-surface. She was getting as bad as him with her wayward speculations.

'Do you want to eat here or by the fire?'

'By the fire, it's more . . .' She stopped suddenly, stunned by what she had nearly said. She'd been about to say 'romantic', which was quite ridiculous—moonlight and roses wouldn't be romantic with him. She was overtired, that was her excuse for such a silly thought. 'More warmer,' she finished as she hastily scooped the bread into a basket to carry through to the sitting room.

'More warmer,' he mused as he picked up the two bowls of soup. 'Are you sure you're features editor of a magazine?'

Verity was glad he went ahead of her and couldn't see her burning cheeks. It was as if he knew what she had nearly said.

The soup warmed and helped to relax her. Rupert had pushed one of the massive black leather sofas closer to the fire, and it was big enough for them to keep a healthy distance between them. Just in case he thought of putting that options remark to the test.

He tossed her an orange from a bowl on the sideboard and sat down again, peeling his and tossing the skin into the blazing fire.

'Dessert. I'm not much of a cook, so I'm afraid you'll have to fend for yourself while you're here.'

While you're here, his voice echoed inside her. 'Wh...what do you mean?' It sounded as if he was expecting her to stay, and not just for the night.

'What I say. I came here for solitude, but if you keep yourself to yourself we shouldn't have a problem. I can't be doing with worrying about when and what you eat.' He turned and his eyes, smoky grey now, raked her up and down. 'Though you look as if someone should be worrying about your health.'

Verity shifted uncomfortably. She was slim, probably thin after that bout of flu, but healthwise she was A-OK.

'It's only for tonight,' she told him, 'so you don't have to worry.' Worry—who did he think he was fooling? He wouldn't even put her mind at ease over Stuart, let alone show genuine concern for her health.

'You don't have to go.'

The suggestion was so unexpected that she swivelled to look at him. He'd finished his orange and
his arm had crept along the back of the sofa, not
nearly close enough to have her worried but something certainly had stirred her awareness. She was
being over-dramatic. So he'd touched her hair,
teased her with that options remark, certainly
nothing she couldn't handle, so why was she so wary
of him?

'No, I can't stay. I want to find out what's going
on, and you're not going to tell me, are you?'

He shook his dark head and the absurd thought
passed through her mind that if she did stay she
might be able to persuade him to be a bit more
forthcoming. Little chance, though. He seemed a
pretty determined sort of specimen.

'I know you don't want to talk about it,' she went
on, 'but at least you could tell me what you meant
by Stuart being perhaps more subtle than you
expected.'

He seemed to mull that over in his mind as he
stared into the flaming fire, and then he turned his
face back to her. 'It just occurred to me that if you
weren't in on this scheme then perhaps Stuart was
trying the softly-softly approach.'

'What do you mean?' Verity hoped she wasn't
sounding too naïve, but she really didn't get the
point.

'The dinner party didn't work, nor did that contrived meeting in the restaurant. I know how desperate your cousin is to get us together. This was
his last resort. Put two people of the opposite sex
together in an isolated environment, far enough

from home for both of them to think twice about flight, and the inevitable will happen—an affair.'

Verity wanted to laugh hysterically. 'Are you out of your mind? We didn't get on before, so we're hardly going to indulge in a raging affair just because we're away from home!' She tore at the peel of the orange she had nearly squeezed the life from as they had talked. 'That's a ridiculous suggestion!'

'So how do you explain both of us being here at the same time, and this place just happening to belong to a friend of Stuart's? No coincidence, Verity. It was his belief that we'd get together intimately, and I don't mean sharing the household chores.'

Horrified, she tossed the uneaten orange into the pit of the fire and shakily stood up.

'Said like that, it's an appalling suggestion.'

'I fear it's the truth,' he told her calmly.

'I fear it's not!' she husked heatedly. 'And how dare you believe that I'm capable of that? You might have shaky morals, but mine are intact.'

'Somebody obviously thinks yours are unstable enough for an affair, otherwise why pitch us together this way?'

Verity's blood was swiftly coming to the boil. Not normally prone to violence, she felt very inclined to slap his head.

'Sit down, Verity,' he calmly ordered. 'And don't be mad with me. *I'm* not suggesting your morals are weak——'

'But you're suggesting Stuart thinks they are?'

'I don't know what he was thinking for sure. I'm only offering up some suppositions. You know him better. What do you believe?'

Verity slumped back down on to the sofa and covered her face with her hands. 'I don't know; I don't know what to believe any more. All the time I thought he was being kind and thoughtful and caring towards me because of Mike's death——'

'Who's Mike?'

Verity uncovered her face and stared into the fire. 'He was my boyfriend, and it was a complex affair and I won't bore you with the details, but he died tragically in a car crash about six months ago. We'd had a row just before he'd driven off and I suppose people felt sorry for me and believed I blamed myself, which I didn't,' she added quickly. 'Stuart thought it his duty to pair me off with a replacement as quick as possible. I thought that was the idea with the dinner party and then the restaurant, just a matchmaking attempt to get me back on my feet.' She faced him and looked into his eyes. 'But... but you seem to think it something more sinister.'

He didn't speak for a long while, and then he said softly, 'I'm sorry, this must be very painful for you.'

'I can cope,' she murmured bravely, tilting her chin defiantly.

'Prove it, then,' he suggested with intrigue.

The flames from the fire were reflected in his eyes and they didn't look half so cold and penetrating, just smoky and mysterious now.

'How?' she asked, her eyes violet and bright with curiosity.

'Stay.'

'For... for what reason?'

'To get on with your work and to prove to your cousin that you aren't the easily seduced woman he thinks you are.'

'He doesn't think that!' Verity shot back hotly. 'He knows me better than that. If he thought I was willing to bed you so easily he would have told me why, got me to go along with this so-called seduction plan to get your damned advertising for him you so hotly believe in.'

'Then the man is an even bigger bastard than I thought,' he drawled dangerously.

Flame burned in Verity's eyes and it had nothing to do with the fire. 'I've had just about enough of this! What the hell have you got against him?'

'Until today, not a lot. Now I see him for the greedy, grasping, selfish bastard that he undoubtedly is.'

Verity tried to get up again, but this time Rupert clasped her tightly by the wrist and held her in place. 'Think about it, just sit still for a couple of minutes and think about it. Your boyfriend is dead. I don't know how deeply you cared about him and I don't want to know, but whatever, it was a relationship and he's gone and it's left you vulnerable. Your loving cousin is very likely working on that vulnerability.'

'How can he be?' she protested.

'He's arranged for us to spend a considerable time together. You're here for a month, me much the same time: long enough for something to develop between us, long enough for temptation to bite into us, long enough to fall in love.'

His voice was soft and low as he spoke, and Verity's heart raced so painfully that it hurt. She couldn't imagine for a minute being in love with him. They were poles apart.

'Love?' she croaked in disbelief. 'We don't even like each other!'

'It's a good start, so the romantics would have us believe.'

'Fantasy with no bearing on true life,' she retorted, 'but that isn't the point. Speaking hypothetically, of course, supposing for a mad moment we were to succumb to temptation and have this affair you seem so ridiculously preoccupied with. How would that help my cousin and my boss?'

'I'm not familiar with the workings of the demented mind,' he grated sardonically, 'but there are two possibilities: blackmail after the event, not for money but for my advertising, although in this day and age not really worth the consideration. The other possibility is even more ludicrous: marriage.'

'Marriage!' Verity exhaled. She shook her head in wonderment at this man's soaring imagination.

'You and I married would be a very acceptable situation for the two of them.'

Verity was speechless. Her mouth dropped open and she stared at him blindly.

'Indeed, the more I think about it, the more I come to believe that that is your cousin's very intention.' His lips tightened. 'Don't look so shocked. I would be a part of your family if we were to be married and I'd be a heel if I didn't give my cousin-in-law my business. It would snowball too. Alan Sargeant is part of the family as well; he would undoubtedly expect some favours.'

Verity remembered an odd remark Alan had made when he had suggested this trip. She had pro-

tested at first, claiming that she was well now and
didn't need a change of scene, especially not so far
away, but Alan had been so persuausive, and when
eventually she had capitulated and told him she
could get the wedding book together in that time
he had said he was sure she could perform miracles
and mysteriously added 'For everyone's sake'. She'd
thought little of it at the time. Was this indeed a
conspiracy? Did those two creeps expect her and
Rupert to fall in love, possibly marry...? It was
too despicable...too horrible for words!

'That's only your interpretation of things,' she
bit out. 'They wouldn't do that to me, they just
wouldn't!'

He said slowly and levelly, 'I'm just offering you
a reason for this, Verity, the only one I can come
up with, I'm afraid. The only way you'll find out
the truth is by asking your cousin and hoping he
gives you an honest answer. But don't be too harsh
on him——'

'Harsh!' Verity flamed. 'This is embarrassing and
unforgivable! That's if it's true, of course!' She had
a feeling it was, though. It was fantastic, but the
only explanation for such subterfuge.

'You said your boyfriend had died; perhaps your
cousin genuinely wants to see you settled with
someone else.'

'And do himself some good too!' she retorted
bitterly. She raked her fingers through her hair and
let out a ragged moan. Stuart had known that her
and Mike's relationship was breaking up but he
cared for her and had tried so hard to make it all
right for her after Mike's death, but this...this went
beyond the boundaries of caring. This would ben-

efit him more than anyone. Of course, it wasn't going to happen, but it left a very sour taste in her mouth.

'I'm sorry,' she said, 'sorry to have subjected you to all this. You're right, this is a family matter and it has nothing to do with you.' She raised her chin proudly. 'I couldn't possibly stay now. I'll leave first thing in the morning.'

'I thought you came here to work.'

'Work!' she spluttered. 'I'm beginning to think the wedding book was just a thin excuse to get me out here. It's been hanging around long enough. To hell with it! I won't do it!'

'You might lose your job over it,' Rupert suggested.

'Job? I won't have a job by the time I've finished telling Alan Sargeant exactly what I think of him.'

'Do you think all this is worth falling out with him over?'

Verity gazed at him incredulously. 'I have some pride, you know!'

'Pride doesn't pay the bills; nor does stubbornness.'

'This has nothing to do with being stubborn. I don't like being used——'

'You haven't been yet,' he interjected reasonably. 'Nothing has happened and it won't if you don't want it to.' He held her eyes, and as she stared at him she realised that he was trying to make it easier for her—and himself of course. He wanted no involvement with her and she wanted even less with him, but he was certainly trying to make her feel better about it.

'What are you trying to say? That I should brave it out?'

He gave a nonchalant shrug. 'I'm willing to.'

'What, stay here together, live together?' she breathed.

'We wouldn't be living together in the sense that your cousin and your boss hope. We'd be living under the same roof, that's all. Providing you keep yourself to yourself, I don't see a problem arising. We both have enough to occupy ourselves with; in fact, we could get away with not catching sight of each other for a month. This place is big enough for that. Are you big enough to give it a try?'

Verity slumped back into the sofa. She wasn't sure, she wasn't at all sure it would work, but for the life of her she didn't know why she had any doubts.

'Stuart and Alan would be sick as parrots if their plan didn't work,' she murmured at last, staring into the fire.

'That's one way of looking at it.'

She gave him a very small smile. 'Revenge, you mean? Stick it out and show that neither of us can be manipulated? I'll go back with my wedding book completed——'

'And your honour intact,' he added with a wry look.

Her smile widened. 'My honour intact,' she echoed. 'Yours too.'

He smiled with her and stretched and then got up. 'While you mull that over I'll make us some coffee, but rest assured, it will be the last I make for you. If this is going to work we each do our own thing.'

'Perhaps we ought to start tonight instead of to-morrow.' As soon as she said it she realised that it was almost an agreement that she would stay.

'No, stay where you are, you're tired. Sugar in your coffee?'

She nodded, and as he moved away she closed her eyes. Yes, she was tired, too tired to make a decision. At this very moment in time she never wanted to see her cousin or Alan again for as long as she lived. She would give in her notice, of course. No way could she work for *Looks Healthy* any more. But Rupert Scott had a point—why give those bastards the satisfaction that their plot might work? And, besides, her job was a good one. Damn, she didn't know what to think, but Rupert was being surprisingly civilised about it all. Perhaps he felt sorry for her; she was certainly the innocent party in all this. She sighed. It could work; it *might* work . . .

She opened her eyes suddenly and he was sitting next to her, closer than before, sipping his coffee and gazing into the dying embers of the fire. She must have dropped off for five minutes and hadn't heard him come back. Her coffee was on the stone-tiled floor next to her and she reached down to pick it up.

'Verity, there is something I think you ought to know about me before we go any further.' He turned to her, and she looked at him with slumbrous eyes. She was so tired, and if he wanted to tell her that he had some strange habits that might disturb her work she would rather hear them to-morrow or, better, not at all.

'Go ahead,' she told him sleepily. 'If you snore and grind your teeth in your sleep, I can survive it. My room is far enough away from yours for it not to keep me awake.'

He didn't smile at that but somehow, without much effort, his face seemed to darken. She remembered that her sort of humour had gone down like a lead balloon at the dinner party. He didn't find her faintly amusing. If this was to work she would have to button her lip if they came into contact at all.

He spoke at last, after draining his coffee and standing up to tower over her. 'I have a lady in my life, Verity,' he told her sombrely.

She looked up at him and for a crazy second didn't think much of his humour either. But this wasn't a joke and she wondered why she had thought it was. She also wondered why he had told her in that warning tone of voice. Was it to put her off or remind himself that he had a commitment to someone else—just in case he was tempted, as the options remark had suggested?

'So? I can live with that,' she returned coldly, surprised at the coolness of her own voice.

'Good. I'm glad,' he said flatly. 'I just thought you should know. Goodnight, Verity. Sleep well.' He turned and walked away, and she stared at the last dying embers of the fire, hearing his tread on the stone steps, the hollow sound of his bedroom door closing behind him.

Verity slowly stood up and shivered. Of course she could live with that; in fact, now she understood why he had made the suggestion that she stay. There was no fear of their having an affair here

because he was already in love with someone else.
Pity Stuart and Alan hadn't checked that out before
arranging all this. But why, then, had he caressed
her hair that way, made that very suggestive remark
which had unnerved her so? She didn't know and
hoped she never would. Attractive he might be; undoubtedly dangerous, though.

Sleep well, he'd said; she doubted that. Too much
had happened, far too much for her to sleep at all
well.

CHAPTER THREE

'TURN that damned thing off!'

Verity scrambled up from the rug on the floor where she was doing her callisthenics and pulled nervously at her pink leotard, horribly embarrassed at being caught so scantily dressed.

Rupert strode into her bedroom and snapped off the ghetto-blaster she'd found downstairs. She'd brought her exercise tapes and Walkman just in case but, finding the blaster, she'd opted to use that for ease.

'I can't have that raucous din when I'm trying to work!' he stormed furiously.

'It's not loud!' Verity protested hotly. 'How can you possibly hear it across your side of the house?'

'Because this damned house is solid stone and every sound ricochets off the walls like bullets. If you must do that ridiculous stuff, have the consideration to do it outside!'

'Outside! It's blowing a gale out there and if we're talking consideration here,' Verity fired back, 'how about you clearing up your breakfast debris after you? The kitchen looked as if a missile had hit when I went down this morning!'

Crikey! Her first morning with him and it had started with him storming into her room in that baggy old tracksuit and attacking her so unfairly. She'd had a bad night, waking at every strange sound of the night. The wind had howled, vixens

45

had screamed, an owl had hooted on the roof and she'd been sure someone had been scraping chains across the stone floors downstairs. The place spooked her and she had been glad Rupert Scott had been within screaming distance. Now this. It wasn't going to work if he was going to be such a slob and so touchy about a little bit of noise.

His grey eyes narrowed warningly. 'Look, we agreed to do our own thing——'

'Within reason!'

'That infernal row in the morning,' he flung his hand out to the blaster, 'isn't within reason!'

'And nor is your dirty dishes littering the kitchen table!'

'That's the way I live when I'm working! Now if you don't like it, clear out and leave me in peace!' He raked his fingers through his already unruly hair and Verity wondered what work he was doing that was causing him such frustration, for if all was going well he wouldn't notice the sounds she was making.

'No way! I'm staying. If you don't like it, *you* clear out!'

They stood glaring at each other, defying each other. He was being totally unreasonable, Verity inwardly flamed. She had purposefully kept the cassette low, but how was she to know that the house acoustics were so bad? Well, she wasn't going to apologise unless he did and if he didn't do something about his washing-up...fat chance! He wasn't the sort of man to stoop to such lowly tasks.

'We'll have to compromise,' she suggested raggedly. It was the only way. Work out some sort of system.

'I'll compromise over nothing!'

'Go hang yourself, then!' Verity shouted furiously at his stubborn arrogance. 'If you're not prepared to bend a little nor am I, apart from my exercise routine, that is!' she added pointedly. With one smart, calculated movement she sprang towards the blaster to snap it back on.

Rupert Scott's reactions were so quick that Verity recoiled back in horror. He grasped her wrist and swung it away from the blaster and pulled her unexpectedly into his arms.

His mouth locked over hers and she was so stunned that she couldn't stop what followed, his lips crushing hers, his tongue easing between her clenched teeth, his arms folding around her body so tightly that she could scarcely catch her breath. She was shocked, too shocked to resist or begin to understand the fierceness of his body hard against hers. She felt his every muscle mould against her, and as his arms slid down to her hips to grasp her into him she was flooded with a searing rush of sexual awareness. Her breasts fought the restricting fabric of her leotard and her pelvis melted against him. His mouth softened as if he knew what his kisses were capable of, as if he knew that the very next step was inevitable.

Verity's mouth parted to emit a small sob of protest under his lips as his hand came up to her breast and caressed the small firm mound. His fingers hardened over her aroused nipple and a sound came from deep in his throat, a terrifying sound of desire.

Verity's heart thundered at what was happening, but her head wouldn't clear enough to reason what to do about it. It simply buzzed out a need, a need that was so fierce and had been aroused so frighteningly easily. And then suddenly it was over. The contact, initially so unexpected, eased away from her, leaving her breathless, frightened and...and oddly empty.

Rupert Scott held her at arm's length and his breath came quickly, as if holding her away from him was causing him pain. His eyelids were heavy and his eyes brittle with anger. His voice was thick when he spoke. 'That wasn't very clever, was it?'

She shook her head in bewilderment. No words came to her lips because her mind was full of only one thought: the unexpected passion he had aroused in her. It had been coaxed so easily by a man she didn't even like very much. At that moment she couldn't help but think of Mike, though she didn't know why.

'Haven't you anything to say for yourself?' he said, his voice in control now.

'It wasn't my fault,' she uttered feebly, lowering her eyes so as not to meet his. She was ashamed of succumbing to that kiss when she should have known better and kicked him in the shins for taking it so daringly.

'Wasn't it?'

She shook her head. 'Don't start that again.' She pulled away from him and snatched up her robe from the bed to slide into it to cover her revealing leotard.

He stood back and watched her. 'The kiss or what?' he teased. How quickly he had regained control when she was still trembling with the shock of what had happened.

'Forget the kiss,' she husked back, 'you know what I mean. I suppose you think I did all this on purpose. Played my cassette at full blast so you would come to my bedroom and I would tempt you into seducing me for that wretched advertising contract for my cousin.'

'I didn't suppose anything of the sort but, now that you mention it, it could be a possibility.' There was mockery in his tone, a teasing mockery that irritated her.

'It isn't! I do this every morning and it isn't a sexual invitation to any passing male.' She looked across to him then, her eyes bright with determination. 'You shouldn't have stormed into my bedroom like that. I refuse to take the blame for what just happened. You were angry with me and that was my punishment, wasn't it?'

'Something like that. If I hadn't kissed you I might have killed you,' he drawled lazily.

'Huh, kiss or kill. I believe you. There are a hell of a lot of men like you around,' Verity sliced back disdainfully.

He frowned. 'Like what? Wanting to appease their frustration and anger with sex?'

Now she knew why her thoughts had spun to Mike. That kiss had reminded her of when their relationship had begun to go wrong. When she had realised she was being used.

'It's obvious your work isn't going well; that's why you're so touchy, and then you switch to punishing me for it,' she husked morosely.

'Was the kiss a punishment? I thought it was just one of those unavoidable accidents.'

'Huh, like slipping on a banana skin!' Verity retorted sarcastically. 'You don't fool me. My last boyfriend used me the same way,' she told Rupert Scott quite openly. 'When life wasn't going easy for him he turned on the sex, his way of blaming me for his own inadequacies. I think you suffer from the same syndrome. He didn't make love to me because he loved me, he just had to prove he was good at something.'

'Was he good?'

The question rattled her. The man had nearly succeeded in making love to her and now he was asking impertinent questions of her as intimately as if it had happened and they were now fully fledged lovers opening up their hearts and their pasts to each other. Well, they weren't and never would be, but she had rather asked for it by mentioning Mike that way.

'I wouldn't know,' she told him defensively. 'I'm not a whore and I don't have a vigorous sex life——'

'So you don't have anyone else to compare him with?'

She held his mocking grey eyes. 'Exactly, and if you've any ideas on supplying me with any comparisons, forget it!' she retorted hotly.

He smiled. 'I wouldn't dream of it. *If* we make love I'd like to be sure it's for the right reasons, not for tallying up the scoreboard.'

'Well, you'll never know, will you?'

'Meaning, you believe we won't make love?'

'Meaning, *if* we did you'd never know if I was chalking up a score for your performance or not!' This was the only way to handle him. Give as good as he expected her to receive. He was pushing her, mocking her, and two could play that duet.

'We might get so desperate that we wouldn't care,' he suggested in that same mocking drawl.

'Speak for yourself! I haven't any problems in that way.'

'Implying I have?'

Verity smiled sweetly at him. 'I'd say you have. You can't keep your hands off me and yet last night you felt the need to tell me you have a lady in your life. I'd say your hormones are niggling at your conscience. Well, I'm no sex therapist, so don't even think about taking what happened just now any further.'

He didn't let up on the teasing smile. 'You could be very right in your pyschoanalysis. My lady doesn't give me any ear drill any more and I find yours sexually stimulating. Keep it up, treasure, and we just might fall into the trap that's been set for us.' With that he turned and left the room.

Verity stared at the back of the door he'd closed after him. So that was a warning, was it? Keep your mouth shut and I won't make any more advances towards you! Or, keep it up and I will! What a choice! She would have to vet every word that came to her lips, and that was going to be quite a strain. But the consequences if she didn't were certainly a deterrent. No problem. She'd just keep out of his way. It was as simple as that!

Verity was cold. Even with a blanket tucked round her legs, she couldn't generate much warmth, nor could the oil-filled electric radiator she'd found in one of the other bedrooms. She'd chosen to work in her bedroom to keep her distance from Rupert Scott, and had set up her computer on the dressing-table. Candice's diets and exercise routines were spread out all over the spare bed. It wasn't the ideal environment to work in but there was no other choice. Downstairs was even colder.

She wondered how he was keeping warm. Better than her, no doubt, in his cosy tracksuit and ex-army boots.

Verity wriggled her toes to get the circulation going and glanced at her watch. Four in the afternoon and so far the day had not been very productive. This morning he had ranted that he couldn't work with the din from her cassette; now she was finding the deathly silence equally irritating. Trouble was, she was listening out for every sound from his quarters. Not that she was remotely interested in what he was doing, she just hadn't wanted to bump into him when she popped downstairs to make lunch or a cup of tea.

She slipped on a jacket and went downstairs. It was a lot warmer outside then in, she discovered when she let herself out of the old mill house. She bared her face to the warmth of the sun and let out a deep breath. She felt better already. Who was she fooling? She sighed deeply. She didn't feel right at all and she knew why she hadn't achieved much all day: her thoughts had wandered down too many leafy lanes of speculation with wretched Rupert Scott for a companion.

That kiss hadn't been too surprising. He might have a lady in his life but she wasn't here, and all men were the same: the first opportunity and they would try it on. Stuart and Alan would have known that, being men themselves. How clever they thought they had been, but she wasn't feeling so clever. That kiss had shaken her for more than one reason. Last night Rupert Scott had convinced her they could handle the situation. Twelve hours later he obviously couldn't, and she wondered about herself. If he hadn't stopped, would she?

Funny, but his mouth hadn't been mean when he had kissed her. It had turned her on. She shivered at the memory of it and turned back from the dirt-track lane she had been wandering aimlessly down and headed back to the mill house.

It was then that she saw him at his bedroom window. Tall, dark, powerfully built and very slightly sinister in the frame of the window. He was watching her. She lowered her violet eyes and carried on back to the house.

'I'm going out tonight. I'll be late. Will you be all right on your own?'

They met on the lower stairs, Verity going up to her room with a scalding mug of tea in her hands, and he coming down, dressed in jeans and a chunky dark green sweater. He was freshly shaved and his hair gleamed in some order and he smelt of cologne.

Verity stood back to let him pass. 'I'd planned on being alone here for a month, don't forget, and don't feel obliged to tell me you're going out for the night. You can manifest yourself into a werewolf and howl through the hills all night, for all I care.' She hadn't intended to sound quite so barbed, but nevertheless it had come out that way.

'I wasn't suggesting you did care, Verity,' he said solemnly. 'I just wanted to know if you'll be all

right on your own. The house is probably more isolated than you expected and——'

'And I'm not an easily scared child,' she told him
sweetly. 'I'm not afraid of the dark or things that
go bump in the night, so off you go.'

She carried on up the stairs, thinking what a little
liar she was. Last night, with a hulk in the house,
she'd been scared. Tonight could be worse; she
would be totally alone. She hoped he didn't plan
on staying out all the night.

Later she lay in bed, waiting, listening to every
creak and groan of the old house. She knew she
wouldn't sleep till he was home. The evening had
been long and unnerving *and* annoying. So they had
agreed to do their own thing, but he might have lit
the fire for her before he'd gone out. She'd struggled
for what seemed like hours to get the kindling going,
and then the big olive logs had refused to ignite and
in a temper she had abandoned it and retired to her
room to work. Cold had driven her into bed at
around eleven, and now at twelve he still wasn't
home!

'You're beginning to think like a wife,' she murmured to herself. She rolled on to her stomach and
buried her face in the pillow. Was his lady his wife?
No, he would have said. A wife would have been
an even bigger deterrent, but perhaps that lady was
going to be his wife and that wouldn't have stopped
him kissing her this morning. He'd been here a week
already and a man had needs . . . Stop it!

Verity sat up, a cold sweat misting her brow, one
of the after-effects of that bout of flu. A cup of
hot tea usually put her to rights. She swung her
long legs out of the bed and reached for the bedside

light. Nothing happened when she flicked the switch. Nothing happened when she tried the main light by the door. Mild panic built up to mania as she lurched across the pitch-dark room and hauled open the curtains at the window. No moon. No light; nothing but the terrifying darkness.

'Don't panic!' she breathed, taking great gulps of air to calm herself. 'There are matches down by the fireplace and candles in the kitchen larder. All you have to do is get downstairs without breaking your neck and find them. Easy.'

Verity lost her footing on the uneven steps the last flight into the sitting-room. She grazed her knees as she pitched forward on to the cold stone floor and bit back tears of frustration at her own stupidity. She should have stayed in bed till daylight—any sensible person would have done that instead of risking life and limb in an unfamiliar setting. She struggled to her feet and touched her knees and let out a cry of pain.

'What the...?'

Verity stiffened in fright, heard the squeak of leather and was aware of movement close by. Someone was in the room!

'Rupert?' Her cry reached the volume of a hysterical scream and echoed terrifyingly loudly in the vast room.

'I'm here; it's OK, I'm here.'

She heard a muffled curse as his foot came in painful contact with the edge of the sofa and then she felt him grip her shoulders, and another cry, this time of relief, tore from her throat as she threw herself into his arms.

Her fingers clawed at his warm, comforting sweater and then wrapped frantically around his neck. Her whole body went into a spasm of violent shaking and, teetering on her toes, she pressed her cold wet cheek to his for comfort.

He held her tightly, securely, his warm mouth brushing her forehead. 'It's all right. There's nothing to be afraid of,' he soothed.

'There's no light,' she whimpered like a small child.

He laughed softly against her. 'I know. The whole village is out. I came back right away. You're terrified.' His hand came up to touch her cheek. She was hot now. 'You've a fever. How old are you?'

Her brow puckered into a frown. 'Twenty-four.'

'Not the menopause, then?'

His attempt at humour brought her down to earth with a bump. He was still holding her tightly with one arm, and she . . . she was still clinging to him like some poor demented soul.

'No, just the after-effects of some antibiotics I've been taking.' She pulled out of his arms in embarrassment. Thank God he couldn't see her face; it was probably scarlet and blotchy, with little to do with the fever. She had thrown herself at him in sheer relief, and he probably thought the worst.

'I'm sorry,' she blurted, 'sorry for throwing myself at you. I was a bit scared and then I fell down the steps.'

'Are you hurt?' He didn't give her a chance to answer but swept her up into his arms and deposited her on to the leather sofa in front of the fireplace. It felt warm through the thin satin of her nightdress, and she supposed he had been lying here in the darkness. The thought unsettled her, more so when he scooped a fleecy blanket round her, and that was warm too. Had he been sleeping here?

'I didn't hear you come in.' She bit her lip; that sounded as if she had been listening out for him. She had, but... 'Rupert?'

His voice called back from the kitchen. 'I'm just getting some candles and firelighters.'

Seconds later he was back with both. 'You must have cat's eyes to see your way around,' Verity remarked.

He lit the candle and placed it on the stone hearth. The small flame momentarily highlighted fatigue in his face. 'I've been here longer than you; I'm used to the place—used to power cuts too.'

'Why didn't you go up to your room, then? You were sleeping down here, weren't you?'

'Does it matter where I sleep?' He gave his attention to the fire.

'Not really, but you look shattered, and bed is the place to sleep.'

'And a place to make love.'

'Sofas make good substitutes too.' She didn't know why she'd said that.

'Is that an offer?'

She gave a small nervous laugh and wished she'd thought before speaking. She tightened the blanket around her. 'No, it wasn't and you know it.'

'I know nothing of the sort. I hardly know you enough to hazard a guess at what's going through your mind.'

'I can see that in future I'll have to be very careful what I say to you.'

'Your energies would be better employed with keeping out of my way altogether,' he said drily.

'Yeah, not so easy when you burst into my bedroom and lurk around down here, waiting for me to fall downstairs.' She tried to inject some light-heartedness into that statement. He really could be quite a sombre and humourless man when he wanted to be, which she thought on reflection was probably most of the time.

'It seems to me you put yourself into these situations on purpose, and I wasn't lurking down here like a crazed psychopath waiting to pounce on you. What were you doing down here anyway?'

The fire suddenly blazed brightly and he sat back on his haunches, staring into the flames. Verity watched him, suppressing yet another sigh. Would he ever believe she wasn't after his body?

'I couldn't sleep, and don't read anything into that. I decided to make some tea, but when I tried the lights there was nothing. I remembered there were candles down here and, well, you know the rest.'

He turned suddenly and looked at her. 'When you threw yourself into my arms you were terrified.'

'Well, wouldn't you be?' she retorted hotly. 'I thought I was alone in the house with no power, and I'd just fallen down the stairs and then I heard this sound. You could have been that crazed psychopath, for all I knew.'

'And you were so relieved it was me——'

'I threw myself into your arms,' she finished for him. 'Very understandable in the circumstances, I'd say—after all, I am a woman.'

'Yes, I suppose so,' he conceded.

'What, suppose I'm a woman?'

He half smiled. 'No doubt in my mind about that, but I meant I suppose it's understandable that you threw yourself into my arms.'

'Oh, I suppose you're well used to it!'

'Thanks for the compliment.'

'I was being sarcastic.'

He turned back to the fire. 'So was I,' he murmured.

Verity's lips thinned with annoyance. 'You're quite a cool cookie, aren't you? I can't imagine you having a lady in your life. I get the distinct impression you don't like them very much.'

'I don't, not since...' He positioned more logs on the fire and she wondered why he didn't finish what he was saying. 'I usually manage quite successfully to ward off preying females,' he went on, 'but some are more persistent then others.'

His words were so loaded that she knew instinctively that he wasn't referring to *his* lady but her!

'May I remind you that I'm not interested in you in any shape, size or form? I've already had a disastrous relationship with one of your species, and I'm not looking for trouble a second time around.'

'Man-hater, are you? That really surprises me.'

From here she could quite easily place her foot between his shoulder-blades and pitch him head first into the fire, but he really wasn't worth the trouble and the mess.

'I must admit to a certain loathing for a certain type—yours. You remind me of my deceased boyfriend, as it happens. He was a miserable, sarcastic moody too.'

He took that, right in the back of the head, and didn't even flinch at her insult, though she had a strong feeling it had hit home. Remorse seized her. He wasn't Mike and to compare the two had been unjust.

'I'm sorry,' she said. 'I shouldn't have said that.'

'Apology accepted,' he said quietly.

He stood up and turned towards her and she wondered if he *had* accepted it. His eyes were unfathomable, his jawline surprisingly tense. She *had* hurt him.

'Any injuries?' he asked.

Her thoughts were diverted by his enquiry and she pulled the blanket off her legs and was dismayed to see that her nightie had risen up over her thighs. She pulled it down quickly but not quick enough for him not to have had a good eyeful of most of her long slim legs. The expression on his face gave nothing away, but nevertheless Verity felt hot with shame.

'Only my knees,' she husked. Both were grazed and one quite swollen and already blue. They didn't hurt any more, so she supposed that there was no structural damage.

'They need bathing,' Rupert told her quietly. 'The floor here isn't too clean.'

He went back to the kitchen before Verity could retaliate by retorting, 'Whose fault's that?'

She leaned back and waited for his return and wished with all her heart she hadn't ventured out of bed—in fact, she wished she'd never come to Spain in the first place. It wasn't working out well at all. But what were her prospects of going back, say, tomorrow? She'd have no job, and a fiery row with her cousin was on the cards, not that she couldn't handle that. They'd practically grown up together and she knew his weaknesses—money and Angie. Though she didn't dislike Angie, she didn't exactly like her either. Angie was a name-dropper, a social climber, the sort of woman who would push her husband to his limits to get the material acquisitions she seemed to thrive on—their enormous house in Barnet, the Porsche, the holidays in Mexico. Verity was beginning to think this very situation was probably engineered by her! She would have to find out.

'You said there's a phone in the village; is it easy to find?' she asked him when he came back with a first-aid kit and a couple of glasses. She wondered what the glasses were for.

'There's a public call box in the plaza, but I'd advise you to use the phone in the Bar Especho. It's metred, so you can pay for it after. There's nothing more offputting than feeding a coin box. I presume you want to phone home.'

'No one at home to call,' she told him, watching as he went to the sideboard and took out a bottle of dubious-looking Spanish brandy. 'I live alone in London. My parents are divorced. My mother lives in Canada with her new husband and my father's a doctor in South Africa and lives with his stethoscope.'

He looked grim. 'I get the picture. I suppose that contributed to the break-up of the marriage.'

'My father's a workaholic and always has been. I don't even know how they got together long enough to produce me.'

He smiled at that and Verity thought he ought to do it more often: it suited him, creased his face in an endearing way. He poured two brandies, put them down on the floor by the sofa, knelt in front of her and clicked open the first-aid box.

'I couldn't boil any water, I'm afraid, no electricity, but there's antiseptic lotion in here. Can you suffer the pain?' He took out cotton wool and upended the bottle to soak it.

Verity realised that he intended to deal with it himself. Her heart contracted at the thought. If she let him he might think it another come-on; if she didn't he'd think any physical contact would be disturbing to her. Strange, but it would. Already she was tensing in anticipation. He dabbed at the graze.

'Ouch,' she cried, 'that stings!'

'Don't be such a baby, it's hardly a scratch. Have a sip of brandy if you're so squeamish.' He reached down to the glass and handed it to her.

'So that's what it's for, to deaden the pain.' She took a sip and shuddered and took another sip.

'Partly. I also thought it might knock you out for the night and we both might get some peace,' he told her drily.

'Very funny!' She gritted her teeth as he dabbed at the other graze, then she gritted every nerve-ending in her body as he gripped her thigh above her knee to hold her still. The effect on her senses was electrifying. She forgot the stinging pain of her knee and the stinging pain of the brandy on her throat. There was only one sensation hurtling through her: his touch on her warm thigh. It was more of a grip than a touch, but the thought of it softening to a sensuous caress had her temperature soaring. No, that's not possible, she reasoned. I must be in shock!

'I think that's good enough,' he murmured, and looked up at her. 'Verity, are you all right?' He took the glass from her clenched fingers and put it down on the floor.

She swallowed, hard. No, she wasn't. She felt sick at what her body was screaming out to her, that she *wanted* his touch to soften, she *wanted* him to caress her intimately. So this morning hadn't been a temporary aberration of her mind. He had aroused her and could so easily do so again, and she didn't really know what she would do if he did.

She held his eyes painfully, and because he didn't take his hand away she knew he knew what she was thinking. His eyes were impenetrable but that mean mouth had softened.

The touch lightened and she thought he was going to pull away, and then very slowly he lowered his head to her thigh. His lips brushed her silky flesh causing a rush of fiery blood to her head, so overwhelmingly that she nearly cried out. His lips lingered, sensuously, then moved higher up her thighs.

'No,' she breathed raggedly, and her hands went jerkily to his head. His hair was soft and unexpectedly silky under her fingers and she wanted to tear at it to hurt him, but instead they coiled into its thickness, drawing him into her. A low groan of pain came to his throat and his hands slid her satin nightie higher and higher, trailing warm, sensuous kisses over her newly exposed skin.

'Rupert, please, don't...'

His head came up at her strangled plea, and as their eyes locked she saw such deep anger that her heart thudded furiously at the injustice of it all.

'Don't look at me like that,' she breathed, pulling her nightie down and trying to get up. 'I'm the one who should be damned furious. How dare you do that to me?'

'Arouse you?' he cried, standing up. 'Have the bloody decency to admit your sexuality instead of trying to hide it with soft, puritanical pleas of no! You want me as much as I want you, so quit the baby-talk.'

She struggled to her feet and faced him angrily. 'Well, our good resolutions didn't last long, did they? How long have we been together in this house...twenty-four, thirty-six, forty-eight hours— oh, who the devil is counting?' Her mind seemed to snap, and furiously she started to unbutton the tiny glass buttons at her breast. 'Let's get it over with now, then perhaps we can both get on with our lives!'

His hands locked over hers, so fiercely that she bit her lower lip. Tears welled in her eyes, blinding her to the sudden softening of his. Her head suddenly cleared and she realised what she had done, and her whole body stiffened with horror and shame. Slowly he drew her into his arms and held her tenderly.

'You didn't mean that, did you?' he breathed into her hair.

'Of course not, you bastard,' she sobbed, so deeply ashamed that she wanted to die. 'Brandy makes me mad as Hades!'

She felt him laugh in her hair and slowly he lifted her chin and lowered his lips to hers. No kiss of passion but one of sweet tenderness, and when it was over he said poignantly, 'Go to bed, Verity, the time isn't right for us yet.'

She didn't question that remark but simply drew away from him without looking at him. As she bent down to pick up the candle to light her way up to bed she knew that something had started, something that might be hard to stop.

Upstairs, confused and weary, she slid back into bed and lay with her eyes wide open. That *something* loomed black and menacing in her mind, blinding her to any sort of coherent thinking. Rupert Scott's lady wasn't much of a deterrent to either of them at the moment, and that was a dangerous thought, even more dangerous than the idea that that awful man was having a devastating effect on her emotional needs. Tonight she had wanted him to love her, or did she just want him to make love to her?

Verity pulled the sheet around her face and bit her lip to stop the tears. She had never felt more lonely and desolate in her life before.

CHAPTER FOUR

So NOW Verity knew why Stuart was so desperate for Rupert Scott's advertising package.

She had let a week pass before making the call to her cousin and probably wouldn't have made it at all if her work had been going well, but it wasn't, and she thought her concern for her cousin was causing the block. It certainly wasn't anything to do with Rupert Scott. She'd convinced herself that vulnerability was a great deceiver of true feelings. She didn't want him—the idea was ridiculous. She was lonely and probably a bit depressed after her illness and that accounted for her silly behaviour on the night of the power cut. Rupert was coping; why couldn't she?

He was being very considerate. No more dirty dishes left lying around; no more sexual overtures; in fact, no contact whatsoever. It it weren't for the diminishing pile of tins in the larder Verity would swear she was the only person occupying El Molino.

For that she should be grateful, but she wasn't. Trying to keep out of his way was getting her down and she was going to have it out with him—that and what Stuart had just told her on the phone.

He was in the kitchen making himself a coffee when she returned from the village, and for that she *was* grateful. He would undoubtedly take it the wrong way if she'd burst into his bedroom.

She plonked the shopping on the table and faced him. 'I've just been to the village and spoken to Stuart on the phone.'

'Was that the first time?' he asked, taking another mug from the cupboard. 'Coffee?'

She nodded. He looked drained and she wondered what he was working on that had kept him locked away for so long. 'Yes. To be honest, I was afraid too call sooner but... well, my work's not going very well and I think I was too preoccupied with wondering at all you had hinted at. Now I know and... and I'm begging you to reconsider, Rupert...'

His eyes blazed suddenly. 'Did he put you up to this?'

'No, he didn't, and after I'd finished with him he wouldn't have dared.' She hadn't gone for the jugular straight away but it was a measure of her cousin's despair when he had broken down almost as soon as she had mentioned Rupert Scott. *Then* she had let rip.

'He's going broke, Rupert, as well you know. His agency is struggling and the banks are calling in his loans and he'll lose his house——'

'Tell his wife to cut down on her silk stockings, then!' he interrupted brutally.

Verity slumped down into a chair and took the coffee he offered. She knew he was right. Angie and her extravagances were bleeding Stuart dry.

'It's not as simple as that,' she murmured. 'He's heavily in debt and your advertising would——' His grip on her shoulder stilled her.

'Listen to me, Verity, because I'm not going to repeat myself.' His voice was low and deliberately pitched so sternly that she knew he meant every word. 'I'm not responsible for your cousin's debts or for the high standard of living that's led him into so much trouble. I've already told you he's not capable of handling my work and nothing you say will change my mind. I don't want him. I don't want Alan Sargeant and I don't want you here if you are going to hassle me every five minutes!'

'I haven't seen you for a week!' she blurted, tempted to sink her teeth into his hand, which was brushing her neck. 'I've only just found out about it and I'm just asking you to give him a chance. Let him do a projection for you... What the hell are you doing?' Suddenly she was being hauled to her feet.

'I'm projecting *you* up to your bedroom, and don't get any fancy ideas that I'm going to bed you. You're going to pack——'

'All right! All right!' Verity cried, twisting so violently in his grip that he let go. 'I won't mention it again!'

He waved a threatening forefinger at her. 'If you do, beware! Remember what happened last time I nearly lost my temper.'

'Kiss or kill,' she murmured, watching him through thick lashes, hating herself for the heat that pulsed through her at the reminder. She rubbed her shoulders where he had gripped them so ferociously.

'Did I hurt you?'

'Some chance! But, seeing as you think you're some sort of commando, do something about this.' She pulled a chicken out from the bag on the table. A *whole* chicken. 'I didn't know how to ask them to top and tail it, and for all I know its insides are still intact.'

He stared at it, lying white and lifeless on the kitchen table, its head to one side, its feet stiff and pointing skyward. 'You want *me* to disembowel it?' He was so aghast that she thought he might have a phobia about such things, but it was more than likely that it was because he thought it beneath him.

'I...I can't,' she murmured. She *did* have a phobia.

'Why buy the damned thing, then?' he shot back.

'I...' Verity shrugged and sat down to drink her coffee. 'I thought I'd cook it—for us,' she added tentatively. 'And don't take that the wrong way,' she blurted quickly as his brow furrowed. 'It isn't an attempt to win you over, it's just that...'

'What?' he urged when she didn't go on.

She stared into her coffee, wishing she hadn't started this. Then she braved herself to look up at him. 'It's just that... I think this is all ridiculous. Us, living like this, avoiding each other. You've been very good this week, clearing up after yourself, making an effort for me. I thought... I thought I'd make an effort too. Cook us a meal——'

'Very dangerous,' he breathed raggedly.

'I'm not that bad a cook,' she tried to joke, and he actually smiled, if thinly.

'You know what I mean,' he said before going to the kitchen drawer and taking out a lethal-looking knife. Verity closed her eyes as he tackled the head and feet of the chicken. She opened them when it was all over.

'Yes, I do know what you mean,' she murmured, 'and I've given it a lot of thought.'

'Have you, now?' he drawled sarcastically, and plunged his hand into the dark interior of the corpse on the table.

'Yes, and I think that we're both being very silly about the whole thing.'

'And what exactly is "the whole thing"?'

'You're not making it very easy for me,' she bleated, studying her coffee once again as he cleaned out the chicken and deposited it into a roasting dish. She waited till he'd washed his hands before going on. 'You've been avoiding me all week.'

'That was the original plan,' he told her drily, leaning back against the work-surface to drink his coffee.

'Well, I think it's silly and childish. We are adults——'

'Precisely.'

Verity let out a long sigh. She wasn't making much headway. She was trying to clear the air and he wasn't helping one bit. 'I didn't like the way you said that,' she told him, 'as if you thought being adults was the whole problem.'

'Isn't it? If we were both children we could handle this situation quite easily. Children don't have the sort of needs we've already displayed to each other. What exactly do you want of me, Verity?'

'Nothing!' Her eyes widened plaintively. 'It's just that I'm not working very well and ... and I think it's because ...'

'Because you want me?' he suggested with such devastating honesty that Verity recoiled with the shock of it.

'No!' she cried, gripping the mug of coffee so tightly that she nearly crushed it. 'I don't want you! I'm just finding avoiding you a bloody nuisance!' she flamed. 'If I want a cup of coffee or something to eat I'm having to creep around like some damned fugitive. Oh, to hell with you!' She stood up and went to leave the kitchen, but he caught her arm and swung her back.

He held her at arm's length but not far enough for her not to be shaken by every *frisson* of awareness that sizzled between them. She had made a mistake, a terrible mistake in bringing this up, because he was misinterpreting her motives.

'You're taking this all the wrong way,' she told him stiffly. 'I just wanted to make my life easier. I can't work with this tension between us and it has nothing to do with what you're thinking.'

'Funny that it took you a week to come to that conclusion,' he bit out. 'Funny that you should bring it up after talking to your cousin.'

Verity wrenched her arms from his grasp. 'I could have put money on you thinking that!' she cried furiously. 'Let's get one thing straight: I'm looking after number one, *my* needs, *my* feelings. Yes, I'm concerned about my cousin's well-being, but whatever you think I'm not trying to soften you up for his sake. I'm doing it for *me*! I can't work because I'm terrified of bumping in to you and rubbing you up the wrong way. I bought that chicken for us because I'm fed up with eating alone . . . not having anyone to talk to . . .'

He gripped her arms again but not half so fiercely. 'When you first came here you expected to be alone.'

'But I'm not!' she sparked back. 'It's different now. I could have coped with being alone somehow but the fact is, you *are* here!'

'That doesn't make sense.'

'Nothing makes sense,' she breathed dramatically. 'I'm just trying to make the best of a bad situation.'

'And your best is cooking chicken for me tonight, knowing what that might lead to?' The depth of meaning in his eyes said it all but she made out that she didn't know anyway.

'Like what?'

'Don't sound so damned naïve. Any enforced intimacy, even over a meal, is very dangerous, Verity, as well you know.'

'No, no, I didn't mean——'

'Like hell you didn't mean,' he grated angrily, his grip tightening. 'Don't be so damned selfish, Verity. All I've heard from you so far is *your* needs, *your* feelings. What about mine?'

'Yours?' she uttered in a hushed whisper.

'Yes, mine!'

He suddenly lowered his head and took her mouth, pulling her so firmly against him that escape was impossible. The pressure of his mouth was crushing, so fierce that her heart leapt with fear, and then slowly, slowly the fear evaporated, exposing all her raw nerve-endings, exposing them to that pressing need deep inside her. The need for someone to hold her and make her forget, someone to love her and make her feel whole again.

The kiss softened into a tempting caress of her sensitive lips, easing away her resistance till she wanted more and more. His arms eased around her, drawing her into his power, running down her body and then crushing her into his sexuality. There was no doubt in her mind of his need at that moment, and how easy to admit to her own. How easy to make love with him, here, now, for the duration of their stay together. And then, after, to return to her empty life and him to return to his lady.

She pulled out from his arms, turned her face up to his and was shocked at the smoky depths of desire in his eyes.

'I don't...don't understand,' she breathed raggedly. 'You want me——'

'Yes, I want you. Why is that so difficult to understand?' he husked, letting his hands drop to his sides.

'You call me selfish,' she whispered defensively, 'but what you are doing is doubly selfish and cruel. Not to me—I'm nothing in your life but a prospective fill-in while you're away from your lady——'

'You object to that?'

Verity's eyes narrowed angrily. 'With every defence in my body,' she breathed heatedly. 'You're despicable, a user——'

'So we're two of a kind!' His voice was terse and punishing.

Verity's mouth dropped open with shock and then snapped shut, only long enough for her wits to rampage wildly. 'Back to Stuart again, eh? You just don't give up, do you?'

'That's where you're very wrong, treasure. You're the one to keep ramming your damned cousin down my throat. At this moment in time Stuart doesn't warrant a mention, because this is between *us* from now on. Don't accuse me of being a user when you're doing the same thing.'

'Oh, yeah, and how do you make that out?'

'Quite simply!' That damned accusing finger of his came up again and Verity wanted to snap it off in fury. 'You have needs, as you so rightly stated, and for God's sake don't come on with that lonely tack again. A cosy dinner for two and a cosy chat, like hell, Verity. Be honest and admit you want the same as me, some warmth, some human contact, some bloody body-bonding!'

'No——'

'Yes!' Rupert insisted so decisively that Verity shuddered with the force of it. She couldn't take his blatant honesty and turned her back on it.

'And that's no way out,' he grated impatiently. 'Face me, Verity, and be honest with me and yourself.'

She swung back at that, her eyes wide with defiance. 'I was being honest with you. I admitted that I'm fed up with having no one to talk to and eating alone, but that isn't enough for you, is it? You want the whole package, my body!'

'What did you expect? Do you really believe it possible that we could live together this way and not end up making love to each other?'

'You said we could.'

'I thought we might, but circumstances change.'

'Nothing's changed!'

'Everything's changed. We want each other——'

Verity shook her head. 'No, you want me! That's the difference!'

'Hypocrite!'

Her anger welled inside her. 'You're being the damned hypocrite. You're the one with someone in your life and you're willing to risk that relationship with a bit on the side—me!'

'And you're trying to lay ghosts. Don't think you fool me with all that rubbish about wanting someone to talk to and being civilised enough to cope with this situation. We want the same thing, Verity: each other. I don't know what you went through with your former boyfriend but whatever it is it's left you with a yawning gap in your life——'

'A gap you think you can fill by making love to me?' she exploded. 'Don't kid yourself, Rupert Scott, you can't do anything for me that another man couldn't!'

'But there isn't any other man available at the moment,' he told her drily.

'And there isn't another woman available for you at the moment either,' she retorted venomously. 'That's why you're so despicable and such a user. I don't have anyone in my life but you have and she isn't here, and you only want me because you miss her!'

Tears burned feverishly in her eyes, tears of anger and dismay at his brutality. But why shed tears over him? And then it hit her why she so desperately wanted to cry: that old vulnerability again, the feeling of loss and failure and insecurity that Mike had endowed her with. He had always made her feel that it was all her fault, undermined her till she had begun to believe that he was right and the reason their relationship had foundered was because she hadn't tried hard enough. This man standing so powerful and strong in front of her was of the same ilk. Well, Mike had nearly destroyed her, but this man wouldn't.

'If you had an ounce of decency in you you'd pack up and get out of here,' she told him flintily.

'And so would you!' he slammed back. 'The fact that you have put up with this all week is a fair indication that you're hanging around waiting for the inevitable to happen!'

Her hand came up to give him that sock in the jaw she had promised, but he caught her wrist and deflected the blow.

'Don't make me mad again, Verity; you know what will happen, or is that the intention? To make me so bloody furious that I'll whip you upstairs and do what we both ache for!'

She twisted her wrist out of his hand and her eyes shot pure poison right between his.

'Go stuff that chicken, because that's the nearest you'll get to any body-bonding while we share this house!'

Verity slammed her bedroom door hard after her and leaned back against it, taking deep breaths to cool herself. She had tried, God only knew how she had tried. All she wanted was some cool, civilised living between them and all he wanted was his own satisfaction! And he had had the audacity to accuse of her of wanting likewise!

She tried to work, stared helplessly at the mountain of sickening diets and boring exercise regimes Candice had prepared for her. Did the bride-to-be really need all this rubbish to make the biggest day of her life worthwhile? Surely the sheer joy of marrying the man she truly loved was enough to bring a glow of radiance to her cheeks, a tingle of sweet anticipation of the wedding-night to hone her body to perfection?

Verity stared at the blank screen of the computer, hugging her shoulders for strength and warmth. She needed something to fire her, needed something to give her inspiration to get on with a job she had no heart for. She tried to project herself as that bride-to-be, to imagine she was preparing to marry, to marry Rupert Scott maybe. Impossible! She didn't even like him, but...there was something there. What on earth was it? A sexual attraction? She wasn't even sure of that. So his kisses turned her on, but his openness shocked her, or maybe it excited her. Maybe he was right and she was still here, hanging around waiting for the inevitable to happen. Oh, God, she didn't know anything any more!

Hunger and cold drove her downstairs when it was dark. She was exhausted but too hungry to take advantage of an early night. She hadn't had a good night's sleep since she had come to El Molino, and those restless nights were taking their toll.

A huge fire blazed in the grate of the sitting-room and there was a delicious smell of roasting chicken coming from the kitchen.

'So you do cook after all,' she said as she stepped into the kitchen. Rupert had just taken the chicken out of the oven, golden roasted chicken surrounded by crispy golden potatoes.

'When I have to,' he murmured, turning to attend to the vegetables bubbling on the hob.

Verity watched him and something inside her softened. He was clumsy and unused to this sort of thing, but he had made an effort and she appreciated that. He'd made an effort with his appearance too. He was dressed in clean jeans and a black roll-necked sweater, and his hair was well groomed. She almost felt guilty for not changing from her warm leggings and purple sweat-shirt to something more soft and feminine. But that would have been dangerous.

'Move over,' she murmured and took the pan from his hands. He didn't object and moved to the cupboard for plates. He'd already set the kitchen table with cutlery. She was glad he'd only done that—a candle, with its soft intimate glow, would have meant trouble.

She jumped when she heard the squeak of a wine cork being drawn and bit her lip.

'Don't panic, this is for me, not you.'

Defiantly she took another wine glass from the shelf and held it out to him. 'I believe in a fair distribution of wealth,' she told him; 'my chicken, your wine, share and share alike.'

He smiled and poured wine into her glass. 'You're not afraid, then?'

She knew what he meant. 'Wine doesn't lower my resistance, just makes me snore, as you'll probably find out in due course.'

He laughed. 'I just might settle for that tonight...' and just when she thought it was going to be all right he added mockingly '...but I won't make any promises.'

Surprisingly, that remark didn't rock her as much as she thought it might. She wondered if she pushed him far enough he might not funk out before she inevitably would.

'This chicken is gorgeous,' she enthused as they sat down to eat.

'Nothing to do with me,' he said modestly. 'It's just a decent chicken.'

'Thank you for cooking it. It was nice of you. Tomorrow it's my turn.'

'So this is going to be a regular routine, is it?' He spooned potatoes on to her plate.

'Why not? We've gone this far——'

'We might as well go all the way,' he finished for her.

Verity sipped more of the wine and decided not to bite back at that. 'Don't put words into my mouth. We've made a start and there's no reason to back down now. I can't see why we can't eat together every night. We both work hard all day and deserve some relaxation. Not the sort that's obviously on your mind morning noon and night, but just a meal and some talk. I'd like to know what you're working on.'

'It wouldn't interest you.'

Verity raised a brow. 'Try me.'

'No way, treasure. It's top secret——'

'And I can't be trusted?'

'It has nothing to do with trust. My emotions are running high enough with you in this house, Verity Brooks, without you putting a witch's curse on my work.'

'Hmm, now you really have whet my appetite. I just might creep into your bedroom while you're otherwise occupied and take a peek.'

'If I catch you in my bedroom I'll make the obvious presumption and act accordingly,' he warned with just a glimmer of humour in his eyes.

'I'll heed that warning,' she told him brightly to show she could take it. 'So if we don't talk about your work, what will we while away the hours with—mine?'

'Remind me; I've forgotten what you said you were here for.'

Verity was inexplicably hurt by that. She watched him eat before saying anything. He was an impenetrable man. She'd thought that the first time she had met him. Hidden depths, a poor excuse for moodiness. So the man had quite an empire to run but was there no room for relaxation in his life? She was forgetting. His mode of relaxation was bedding. She could just imagine the sort of lover he would be—wham-bam-thank-you-ma'am, excuse me while I get up and make another million while you're recovering!

'The wedding book,' she told him offhandedly to cover her hurt. 'Diets and exercises to prepare the bride for a life of wedded bliss.'

'Ah, yes, I remember now. What some people will do for a buck, I thought at the time you mentioned it,' he said derisively.

'It wasn't my idea,' Verity retaliated. 'It's one of Alan's money-spinning ventures. It's giving me some trouble, though,' she admitted. 'It's dragging its weary train up the aisle at snail's pace.'

'I'm afraid I can't help you there. I'm not very successful at the wedded-bliss game,' he told her with such coldness that Verity nearly dropped her fork with surprise. For some reason a cold chill ran up and down her spine. The lady in his life—was she his wife? Dear God, he was married! Not successfully, though, by the sound of it.

'You sound cynical about marriage,' she ventured, too afraid to ask him outright if he was or wasn't married.

'And what do you think of it?' he asked, cleverly getting out of giving her an answer, though it had hardly been a direct question.

'I believe in it. If two people truly love each other it's inevitable.'

'Did you expect to marry your boyfriend?'

Verity's eyes levelled with his. She had asked for this, wanting to shift their relationship to a more convivial level, and this was the result. Oh, well, if she opened up he might. She was madly curious to hear about his wife.

'I didn't love him,' she answered truthfully.

'Yet you were having sex with him, and there was I, thinking you were a little puritan at heart.'

Verity dammed a blush before it flooded her face. So he hadn't remembered much about the book she was working on, but there was nothing wrong with his memory where her sex life was concerned!

'I liked him a lot when we started going out with each other. You don't have to love a person to want to go to bed with them.'

His dark brow went up at that. He said nothing but she sensed what was going through his mind. If those were her views and morals, why hadn't she leapt into bed with him?

'I hoped it would lead to love,' she went on hurriedly. 'I cared enough for him to want him to make love to me. I thought that once we were actually lovers it might prove that I actually was in love with him but if I wasn't it might deepen into love. I made a wrong calculation, a mistake. I ended up being used.'

'And you're still very bitter about that?' He leaned back in his chair, the meal finished, the dessert, her confessions, making her squirm in her seat.

'Yes,' she whispered. 'With myself more than anyone. I made a mess of the whole affair.' She levelled her eyes at his and he held them and she thought he would understand. 'I made mistakes and then couldn't rectify them. I didn't know how to handle him or how to get out of it. He was a graphic artist and in the wrong job and he wasn't happy. I couldn't help him and he made me think it was my fault. When he died it was as if he had done it to punish me.'

'He committed suicide?'

Verity shrugged her narrow shoulders. 'I'll never know. We had rowed for the umpteenth time and he went out drinking and headed up north. There was a motorway pile-up...and...and he died. It was foggy——'

'So it was more than likely just an accident,' Rupert volunteered quietly.

Verity shrugged. 'I try to convince myself that it was an accident, but there will always be a doubt.'

'You can't go on living like that, though. You've to get on with your life.' He didn't sound as if he was very convinced of that advice himself, and Verity frowned slightly.

'Oh, I have,' she insisted. 'I can't change what's happened but...well, it's made me wary, unsure of myself where personal relationships are concerned.'

'And you don't want to make the same mistake twice?'

'Something like that.'

'It might surprise you to hear that I wholly endorse that.'

So he did have a murky past he was trying to live with. Perhaps a painful divorce, or possibly one coming up!

Verity gave him a watery smile. 'If there is ever a next time for me I want to be absolutely sure the man is as committed to me as I would be to him. A good, honest, down-to-earth relationship with no holds barred.'

'Equal partners in the love game,' he mused with a cynical laugh. 'Asking a bit much, aren't you?'

He grated his chair back and got up to put the kettle on, and Verity watched him through narrowed eyes. He looked so sombre that she wondered what had happened in his life for him to be such a cynic. That painful-divorce theory loomed larger than life now.

'I don't think so,' she told him warily. 'At least I'm looking on the positive side of marriage.'

'You're seeking perfection, which is totally unrealistic in this day and age.'

Verity bridled. 'And you're preoccupied with the imperfect side of it. Just because yours didn't work, it doesn't mean——'

'My what didn't work?' he questioned stonily, turning to face her.

'Your... your marriage.'

'I don't recall mentioning I was married.'

'You didn't but you said you had a lady in your life and... and you're pretty cynical about marriage *and* you just said you weren't very successful at wedded bliss.'

'All very true,' he admitted in an unforthcoming manner, and turned back to making the coffee.

'Now who's turning their back,' she said pointedly. 'Face me, Rupert,' she mimicked, 'and be honest with me and yourself.'

He swung round then, so ablaze with anger, his eyes so threatening and intense with rage that she nearly ran for her life.

'Just what the hell do you want from me?' he rasped furiously.

In that moment Verity wasn't at all sure why she was doing this, pushing him to reveal something of himself, something he was loath to open up to. Her mind flash-fired everything she knew about him, and one thought flamed above all others: the picture of him dining alone in that Knightsbridge restaurant; a lonely man. She hadn't seen it before, not till now.

'I'm sorry,' she murmured, lowering her lashes. 'I...I don't want anything from you...I just thought...' She took a deep breath and looked up at him, her violet eyes wide open. 'It helps to talk,' she murmured.

'It hasn't helped you much, has it?' he said frostily. 'You're still carrying your boyfriend's death around like spare emotional baggage.'

Shakily Verity got to her feet. 'I've tried,' she told him levelly. 'Which is more than you're doing. I don't know what your problem is but I know what you think the answer is—to bury yourself out here and hope when you surface the nasty gremlins will have run away. Life ain't that predictable,' she spiked bitterly. 'If I were you I'd go back to this lady of yours and bed her instead of me! I'm no damned substitute for the real thing!'

He caught her as she reached the archway to the sitting-room. He pinned her to the wall, holding her wrists above her head. She smelt the wine on his breath and his cologne and in that instant wondered why he had bothered, and then knew, knew what the whole evening was about, cooking for her, making an effort with his appearance: he wanted her and fully intended it to be tonight.

'You are the real thing,' he rapped urgently. 'Flesh and blood——'

'For the moment!' she grazed back bitterly. 'A warm body to take the place of your lady till you get back and pick up your flagging wedded bliss!' She tried to twist her wrists free but they burned painfully.

'They do say that an affair can sometimes resurrect an ailing relationship,' he mocked.

'So that's what all this is about, is it? By seducing me it might make you realise what a little *treasure* you have at home.'

'I know precisely what I have at home: fifteen empty rooms with the lingering scent of my lady's perfume . . .'

Verity's whole body stiffened. So he was married and she'd left him! She didn't want to hear any more, she just didn't.

'Let go of me!'

'When I'm good and ready.' His lips were hot and angry on hers, punishing her for that wife of his who'd left him. Verity boiled with rage and the injustice of it all. She squirmed and battled under the assault of his desire but the pressure of his mouth softened, with deadly expertise, the fight that blazed inside her. Slowly, fatally, he worked on her lips till she felt the well of her own desire rise inside her. He let go of her wrists and her arms dropped weakly to her sides and she clenched her fists tightly in a desperate attempt to hate him.

His mouth moved from hers, fluttered across her jawline and down to the small hollow of her throat. His hands moved round her hips, moulding her into him, then, satisfied that she wouldn't struggle any more, he slid them under her sweat-shirt, beaming up to her naked breasts, so smoothly as if they were programmed for that very purpose.

To her shock, his fingers trembled on her nipples, only for an instant, as if he was unsure, and then he was in control again, circling her breasts, teasing her nipples till her whole body flamed with liquid heat.

But it was that small unsure tremble that had the deepest effect on Verity. He didn't even care for her. Just like Mike, he was trying to prove a point. Rupert loved his wife and she had left him, and she, Verity Brooks, was the woman who would prove that he wasn't the failure he thought he was.

She brought her hands up then and pressed them hard against his chest. He didn't take much persuading to pull back from her. He stepped back and those smoky grey eyes were unfathomable again.

Verity's brimmed with unshed tears, for in that moment she knew that she wanted him. She wasn't sure how deeply or intense the need for him was, but what she did know was that if it were a different place in different circumstances she would want this man in her life. To love her, to make love to her, to give her all she lacked in her life. But it was an impossible dream, as impossible as speculating for sure what had been in Mike's mind when he had taken off for that foggy motorway.

Without a word, a look, a gesture, she turned away from Rupert Scott and walked resolutely away from him.

CHAPTER FIVE

VERITY'S work took off with a vengeance the next day. She worked feverishly, determinedly. It was the only way. Rupert was married, not happily; he still loved his wife; she'd left him; he wasn't coping... A knock on her bedroom door had her jerking with fright.

'Come in.' She turned from the computer as Rupert stepped into the room. 'How very civilised, knocking now. What happened to the SAS approach?'

'Sarcasm is the lowest form of wit,' he drawled. 'Can I borrow your car?'

'Why?'

'It's raining and I don't want to get wet.'

She turned back to the computer. 'Why haven't you got a car of your own?'

She heard a rasp of impatience come from deep in his throat. 'I wanted total isolation. I took a taxi from the airport and I'll take a taxi back. I need to go to the village to make some phone calls; now do I get the car or do I get wet?'

She was tempted to shoot back 'Get wet' but didn't. 'The keys are downstairs on the shelf next to the glasses.' Without turning, she said, 'While you're out, get some fresh bread and some salad, and I think we're out of milk.'

'What did your last slave die of, battle fatigue?'

'Sarcasm is the lowest form of wit,' she echoed brightly as he slammed the door after him.

She stared at the window after he'd gone. She hadn't noticed the rain and the wind howling and rattling the ill-fitting grilles on the windows. She saw it now, felt the chill of the room close in around her. She hated it when he wasn't here, though this was only the second time it had happened. But it was daylight and she wasn't afraid, just sort of... She shrugged; she really didn't know.

An hour later he still wasn't back. She hadn't done much in that time. He'd distracted her by coming into her bedroom, and since then she'd been too preoccupied with him and all that had happened last night. She got up from the computer and moved restlessly out of her room, across the landing and into his.

It was tidy, although she wasn't checking up on him. But what was she doing in his bedroom? She didn't know, but she was here and standing in front of his computer. She wondered at her nerve as she loaded it and then slid in the nearest disk to hand.

'Surprise, surprise,' she murmured after a while, and picked up the book he was working from. She flicked through it, put it down and picked up his notes.

'You surprise *me*,' a cold voice came from the door.

Shakily Verity turned to the door, scarlet in the face by the time she faced Rupert fully. He stood in the doorway, watching her, his hair wet and his features tense.

Though his voice was cold and his words mild, she knew he was red mad with her. His narrowed, steely eyes indicated the intensity of his control over that fury.

'I'm sorry. I didn't mean to snoop.'

He came towards her and ejected the disk from his machine. 'And this loaded itself, did it?' he grazed sarcastically.

'Of course it didn't,' she retaliated quickly. There was no defence, none at all, and she didn't attempt it. 'I was curious to see what you were working on.'

'You could have asked me——'

'I did. You wouldn't tell me.'

'So you just waited till I was out and then sneaked in here and invaded my privacy.' His voice was so thick with contempt that Verity wished she had kept away. 'That does surprise me, Verity; I was beginning to think you weren't a typical female.'

Her colour had returned to normal and she drew her chin up. 'Well, I suppose this proves I am. I'm not denying it. I was crazy with curiosity.'

'And you know what happened to the cat who was too curious?' He slid his notes and the book into the top drawer, out of her way.

'Are you going to kill me?' she murmured, half teasingly.

He held her eyes and she knew her attempt at humour wasn't going to abate his anger.

'Perhaps you're angling for the alternative.' His eyes seemed to darken more, if that was possible. 'Remember what I said about catching you in my room?'

Verity bit her lip. She had forgotten his threat and what he would assume if he did find her here.

'I didn't, I honestly didn't come here . . . for . . .'

'For sex?' His black brows winged. 'Hardly—I wasn't here. But now I am,' he added meaningfully.

Verity took a step back and then another. 'Don't make threats like that, Rupert,' she murmured.

He didn't say anything, which surprised her. She would have thought something mocking would have tripped from his lips.

'I'm sorry,' she offered once again. 'I didn't mean to invade your privacy...' She let out a small sigh. 'That's silly; yes, I did, I suppose, but...but I didn't expect to get caught.'

Rupert leaned back agains the desk. 'Well, that's honest,' he grated, 'but doesn't alter the fact that you did it and I'm not very pleased about it.'

'Why?' Verity asked. She knew she ought to be high-tailing it out of here but that wretched curiosity of hers was pinning her to the spot. The contents of that disk she had loaded had hooked her.

'It's personal.'

'What is? *Molly Shaw*? There's nothing personal about that. The book is a classic.'

'You really have been snooping pretty hard, haven't you? Did you sneak in here as soon as I'd left?'

'No!' Verity exclaimed. Her hand went up to rake her hair from her face. 'Look, I didn't meant to. I was just restless, waiting for you to come back, and I wandered in here and honestly, I don't know why I did it. I just loaded your machine up and read a bit of your work. I mean, I don't even know what it's about...what exactly you are doing...'

'A screenplay, an adaption of *Molly Shaw* for the big screen.'

'Oh,' Verity breathed. She hadn't been sure, she had suspected it was something like that, but, 'I...I didn't know you were a writer,' she said.

'I'm not.'

'Oh,' she breathed again, trying to understand, and then suddenly she did. She smiled. 'I do understand, you know. Childhood ambitions and all that. I used to want to be a ballet dancer but I didn't have what it takes...'

'This isn't a childhood amibition,' he told her curtly.

'Oh——'

'And will you stop breathing ''Oh'' like that?'

Verity shrugged. 'I'm sorry. It's just that I'm surprised. I thought you were a businessman and presumed you were working on some accounting or something. A screenplay,' she murmured, fishing for more. 'I'm very impressed.'

'I doubt that,' he grated. 'Now would you like to leave so that I can get on with it in peace?'

'Why doubt that I'm impressed?' Verity urged. She didn't want to go yet.

His eyes locked into hers. 'Are you really interested or are you just making conversation? In my bedroom?' he added meaningfully.

Verity shifted her feet but held her ground. 'I'm not interested in what you think I'm here for because it isn't true, but I'm very interested in your work. I'm loosely a writer too, nothing as impressive as a screenplay, but you never know what the wedding book could lead to.'

He smiled at that but offered no more and went over to the bathroom to get a towel for his wet hair.

'Is it still raining?' she asked. Silly question when it was obvious it was, but she was making conversation because she wanted to hear more about his work.

He stopped rubbing his head and looked at her coolly. 'Get out, Verity.'

The tone of his voice and the way the words were delivered with such deep warning affected her. She felt it as sharply as if he had pricked her with a hot needle. Suddenly something sheered off the walls, nothing you could put a name to, just a charged feeling of awareness of each other. Nervously Verity stepped back, not taking her eyes off him for an instant. He didn't move, just stood poised with his hands stilled on the towel and his damp hair, watching her, testing her, daring her.

Verity turned and fled.

She was making tea when he joined her in the kitchen, and probably because it was the kitchen there wasn't a repetition of that buzzy sexual awareness.

'I got the shopping you asked for,' he told her.

'Yes, thank you. It's my turn to cook tonight. Do you like spaghetti?'

'Fine by me.'

He sat down at the kitchen table and she made the tea without speaking. She wondered why he was sitting there when he had lost a good part of the working day already.

'Is it easy to adapt a book for the screen?' she asked.

'Depends.'

'On what? How good you are?'

He smiled and took the cup of tea she offered. 'You really are intent on getting it out of me, aren't you?'

Verity sat at the table. 'It interests me, really it does. You have your own film company. Are you intending to produce it yourself?'

He nodded. 'And direct it.'

'And star in it?' Verity teased.

'Hardly. I'm not into drag. It's the story of a mother who raised seven daughters single-handed during the industrial revolution.'

'I know,' Verity smiled. 'I have read it.'

'Do you think it will make a good film?'

Verity was flattered that he wanted her opinion. 'I'm surprised it hasn't been done before and surprised you're tackling it personally.'

'I didn't intend to. I mean I intended to produce it but the team of writers I hired were hopeless.'

'So you thought you'd have a go yourself?'

He nodded. 'My father was a writer—Alex Scott; heard of him?'

'*The Shardfords* and the *Cumbrian Trilogy*.' Verity was impressed.

'I thought some of his talent might have rubbed off.'

'From what I read on your disk, I believe it has, and I'm not just saying that to make up for snooping on you.'

'Thanks,' Rupert murmured, and smiled. 'I'm sorry if I was a bit cross with you for intruding, but I must admit to a certain reservation with this part of my work. Sarah was very derisive——'

'Sarah?' Verity interjected quietly. Her fingers coiled round her cup. 'Your wife?'

'The lady that was nearly my wife. We lived together for two years. She walked out six months ago.'

Desperately Verity tried to appreciate the fact that he wasn't married but it wasn't easy. Sarah might not have been his wife, but Verity could read in Rupert's eyes the depth of his loss.

'Didn't she like the thought of you being a writer?' Verity realised she had forced that out, striving for some sort of normality though she wondered why the need. What did it matter, his ex-lover's opinions?

'She didn't like anything that took up my time. A very possessive lady.' He grated his chair back and the sound matched his voice. 'What time's dinner?'

'About eight.'

He went back upstairs and Verity was left alone with her thoughts. She cleared up the dirty cups and wondered why Sarah had left him if she was such a 'possessive lady'. Suddenly she smiled to herself. A week ago she wouldn't have had any doubt in her mind why any woman would want to walk out on such a morose, arrogant swine, but now . . . She shrugged. What had changed? He was still a morose, arrogant swine. Sexy with it, though, she conceded.

She went back upstairs to her bedroom. She had another couple of hours of working time but it was colder than ever. She peered down at the radiator and turned the setting up to maximum. It was then that the lights blew, and there was a flash from where the radiator was plugged in.

Verity screeched so loudly that she thought Rupert must surely hear. She rushed to her door to shout that she was all right, but he was already bearing down on her.

'What the hell have you done?' He thrust past her and wrenched the radiator plug from its socket. 'You've blown all the electrics!'

'*I've* blown all the electrics? How do you make that out?'

'You've got the damned thing plugged into a lamp socket.' He pointed to another plug-point across the room. 'You should have used that one, a heavy-duty plug-point.'

'Well, I'm not a damned electrician. How was I supposed to know the workings of Spanish electricity? It's been working perfectly on that,' Verity protested, waving her hands at the connector. 'There's something wrong with the radiator, there must be. I turned it up——'

'And overloaded the circuit,' he growled at her.

'But I might have been killed!' she wailed, distressed that he wasn't concerned for her safety.

'But you weren't and I've lost precious work on my computer because of the loss of power!' he slammed back at her.

Verity's shoulders sagged. 'I'm sorry,' she murmured. Oh, God, she knew how she would feel if it had happened to her.

'Like hell you are!'

'I am!' she screamed. 'Just remember my name's Verity, not bloody Sarah!' As soon as it was out she wished it was in. Her teeth clamped over her bottom lip in remorse.

'I can live without you, Verity Brooks,' he grated harshly after freezing her to the spot with the blackest of looks. 'I can live very well without you!'

He slammed her door after him. It was minutes before Verity moved and then only because the lights had flashed back on. Whatever he'd done, he'd fixed it. She wheeled the radiator across the room and plugged it into the socket he had suggested. It didn't work, but at least the lights hadn't blown again.

She didn't knock on his bedroom door but marched straight in. 'I'm truly sorry about what happened. It wasn't done intentionally.'

'I know,' he drawled, and turned from his computer to face her.

'And I'm sorry about what I said about Sarah. It was awful of me.'

'It was,' he agreed.

She stepped towards him. 'Did you lose much?'

He turned back to the computer. 'Not much, but enough to make me as mad as hell.'

Verity smiled and reached out and touched his shoulder, and the touch turned to a caress and she was amazed at her own audacity in touching him so intimately.

'Don't do that, Verity,' he warned without turning. 'I won't be responsible.'

Verity stilled her hand but didn't remove it. She knew then that she didn't want him to be responsible at all. She wanted him to turn and take her in his arms and forget Sarah and have only Verity Brooks in his heart.

Did he read minds too? He turned and slid his arms around her waist and she bent her head and buried her mouth in his thick hair.

'I'm sorry too,' he rasped. 'I should have shown more concern for you. Did you get a shock from the radiator?'

'Only one of fright,' she whispered back, but she was more afraid now. He slid her sweat-shirt up and grazed his mouth tantalisingly across her bare midriff. Verity let out a small gasp of sheer pleasure. Her mind accelerated, taking her further and further in her sea of imagination. She was naked with him and he was loving her, kissing her, about to consummate what she so longed for. He was loving her, making love to her, entering her and . . . mouthing the name Sarah as he did it.

Her body stiffened, her heated flesh cooled desperately quickly. She tried to pull away, but he held her.

'Don't tease, Verity. I don't like that,' he husked achingly.

He stood up as she tore herself away. He reached her at the door, swung her back and kicked shut the door.

'I said I don't like that, Verity. Don't start something you don't intend to finish.'

'I shouldn't have come. I just wanted to say I was sorry,' she uttered weakly as his hands pinned her to the door by her shoulders.

'And offer your body in payment and then draw back when you had second thoughts?'

She didn't answer, just stared at him, stupefied. Why had she come? She knew; deep in her heart, she knew.

'It . . . it wasn't second thoughts.'

'What, then?'

'You're clever at reading my thoughts. I'd thought it was obvious.'

He graced her with a cynical smile. 'The lady in my life?'

Again she offered nothing. Again he smiled cynically. 'And what about the lost lover in your heart, Verity?'

She shook her head. 'I never loved him, and he's dead now anyway. You loved your lady and she's still with you, you said that; you said she was in your life . . . so you must still love her.'

'And what the hell has love to do with us? Don't tell me it's a consideration here?'

Her whole body burned in his grasp. She squirmed, but it was useless to try to free herself.

'No, it's not a consideration!' she breathed heatedly. 'But I'm no substitute for your lost lover and that's what I would be if we did make love. You've never shown any feelings for me before——'

'And I'm sure the feeling is damned mutual!'

'My God,' Verity gasped. 'Stuart was right—put two people in an isolated situation and sex will rear its ugly head.'

'Sex is ugly to you, is it?' he asked derisively.

'I didn't say that . . . but yes . . . yes, it damn well is when it's used this way!'

He lowered his lips and let them brush dazedly across hers. 'This is ugly, is it?' His body, warm and inviting and very aroused, was crushed against hers.

Dear God, but it was the opposite. Beautiful and tempting.

'Don't——'

'Don't,' he echoed against the paleness of her throat. 'That's all I ever get from you, Verity Brooks. Why don't you try "do" for size and see how you like it.'

'Not this way!' she cried, struggling in his grip, but when his mouth took hers again the struggle faded away. There were tears in her eyes because this was all so reminiscent of what she had been through before. Mike punishing her for his inadequecies, and now Rupert punishing her for Sarah's.

She wanted him to stop this assault on her tender emotions. She wasn't ready for this, to just give herself to him in the heat of the moment, just because she was so desperately lonely and so was he.

With a mammoth effort she was out of his arms and wrenching at the door-handle. To her surprise, he stood back and opened the door for her. His eyes locked her out, staring down at her as she hesitated in the doorway. They were cold and hostile and she returned that hostility with her own cool violet eyes.

'I came here to apologise and it stands. I haven't changed my mind.'

'Will you ever change your mind?' he husked.

She didn't even question about what, because she knew. She didn't answer yes or no either, but that was because she didn't know.

She tried to work but it was impossible, so she went downstairs and struggled with the fire till she had it blazing. She sat back on her heels and watched the flames fiercely gather momentum. She presumed Rupert was still upstairs working. It was getting dark and she ought to be thinking of getting the dinner on, but she was loath to leave the fire and loath to make that final decision. Did she want to let go and allow this affair to happen? She liked him enough to, but she had been hurt and used before and so had he, and was just liking enough? She bit her lip and realised that that was just the decision she'd had to make with Mike. She hadn't loved Mike but had hoped the intimate side of their relationship would develop that liking into love.

'What are you thinking?' Rupert asked as he came down the stone steps into the sitting-room.

Verity didn't get up and Rupert came and sat behind her on the sofa. He reached out and loosened her long blonde hair from where it was caught in the collar of her sweater.

'I was thinking about relationships,' she told him quietly, staring into the fire.

He laughed softly. 'Your honesty is one of the things I like about you. Any other woman would have said something inane like "nothing in particular". There isn't a second of your life when you think of "nothing in particular".'

'Would Sarah have said that?'

'Yes. She wasn't honest like you.'

'Why did she leave you?' She turned then to look at him. His eyes were dark and broody and she sensed he might not tell her. Men were worse than women for hiding their true feelings.

'I didn't give her enough of my time. Sarah was a very demanding lady.'

She sounded like Mike, Verity mused. 'You loved her very much, didn't you?'

To her surprise, he shook his head and the corners of his mouth turned up. 'Not enough. If I'd loved her more I wouldn't have left her alone so much, would I?'

Verity shrugged. 'I don't know. Maybe you didn't realise quite how much you loved her till after she'd gone.'

'Maybe.'

That wasn't what Verity wanted to hear. She looked away from him and stared into the fire again. 'I got the impression you were choked off with her leaving you.'

She heard a soft laugh behind her and swung round again. 'What's so amusing?'

'You. You're determined to get it all out of me, aren't you?'

Verity coloured and lowered her lashes. 'I'm just curious.'

'You are,' he agreed, 'but I wonder for what reason.'

Her eyes widened. She wondered herself, but not for long. Of course she wanted to know his feelings before letting herself go. She didn't want to be hurt again.

She scrambled to her feet. 'I'll get on with the dinner.' She hurried out of the room and he didn't follow her. She worked feverishly on the meal, amazed at the thoughts that swept in and out of her mind. She was actually considering having an affair with that man and wanting to get the clutter of his past relationship with Sarah, a woman she didn't know or want to, out of the way. She was mad, quite mad, because what difference would it make? An affair was an affair and didn't spell anything more.

She had to go through and get him when he didn't respond to her call that dinner was ready.

He was asleep, stretched out on the sofa. The fire was dying down and she jammed a couple more logs on the embers. Then she turned and studied him. He was tempting. So strong and powerful and very good-looking. His hair was in need of a cut and somehow that made him more appealing than when she had first met him. Then he had been suave and sophisticated and quite aloof; now he was human. Sarah had been a fool. To be living with this man and to have lost him. She should have stood her ground and fought for his attention.

'That's what I would have done,' Verity murmured as she reached down and touched his shoulder.

'What was that?' he muttered, opening his eyes fully.

'Supper's ready.' She smiled and flicked a wisp of hair from his brow in a playful gesture, and he caught her wrist and pulled her down on top of him.

'How much longer are you going to hold me off?' he drawled against her silky hair.

'I wasn't aware I was,' she murmured back.

'That sounds very interesting, very interesting indeed.'

'And so is my spaghetti,' she teased. 'I improvised a bit but I'm sure you'll like it.'

'Do you improvise in bed too?'

'You'll probably never know.'

'Only probably, so there is still hope,' he teased, running his hand up and down her back.

'Very little,' she murmured, and suddenly knew that to be true. She did want him and there was no doubt he wanted her, but only while they were here in this isolated mill house. Then the affair would be over and they would return to their lives. So what more did she want? Disturbed by that thought, she tried to get up from his lap.

'Not so fast.' His hand locked around the back of her neck and he pulled her down to him. The kiss was incredible. Powerful and promising, and the temptation surged urgently inside her. She responded because she could do little else. Her lips parted, her hands slid over his shoulders. His warmth and smell engulfed her, tempting her further and further down into his sexuality.

He moved and swivelled her round so she was lying on the sofa and he was straddled across her. His head was above hers and he gazed down into her eyes.

'Do you mean that, that we have little chance of coming together?'

She bit her lip and couldn't answer. How did she know? Today was today, tomorrow tomorrow. If he kept up those kisses, who knew where it would lead?

He smiled as if knowing her hesitation. 'It will have to be your choice——'

'That's not fair!'

His brows rose darkly. 'I think it's very fair. You know I want you, so you're not going to get a fight from me. But I'm not going to force myself on you,' he grinned suddenly, 'unless, of course, that's what you want.'

'Violence?' she husked, aghast. 'You wouldn't?'

'I wouldn't,' he smiled, 'but you do rather tempt me at times. Now it's my turn to be honest with you. I want to make love to you. I want an affair with you, but I warn you, I'm not very good at relationships.'

Verity smiled cynically. 'So you're offering an imperfect affair, no strings, no pain. Straight sex and when our time is up——'

'We more than likely go our separate ways,' he finished for her.

She started to laugh then, and her body shook under his. 'Well, I've had some propositions in my time but that takes the biscuit. Sarah did the right thing by walking away from such blatant chauvinism.'

He stiffened against her and then sat up. Verity swung her legs over the sofa and stood up.

'I suppose you thought you were being very nineties by making a statement like that?' she asked him, though it was more of a statement than a question.

His dark eyes held hers. 'I said it, Verity, because it's how I feel. I've had one sour relationship which I don't want to repeat——'

'So you're afraid? Well, so am I,' she told him levelly. 'But that gets you nowhere in life. Some time you'll have to take the plunge with another woman, but with that dour warning at the beginning of things I'll doubt you'll ever get further than a one-night stand.'

'So you are a typical female after all. Making demands and expecting hearts and roses and wedding bells from the off.'

'I didn't say that. I'd be quite willing to live with a man if I cared for him enough, and I'd have an affair if I cared and wanted enough.'

'So why this argument? Do you care enough for me to take on an affair with me?'

'I . . . I . . .'

'You don't know, do you? You're putting up barriers before you even know what's going on in your own mind. You do want me, you do want an affair, but you're as scared as I am.'

'Of course I am. I've already said I am. I've had a rotten relationship too and I'm wary, but at least my heart is open to offers. Yours isn't. Sarah still lies bleeding in yours and not because you really cared for her but because your bloody pride was stung because she walked out on you!'

She went to skirt the sofa and he reached for her, tenderly, which surprised her. His hands smoothed down her upper arms.

'You're very right,' he said quietly. 'I failed in a relationship and that isn't anything to be proud of. I can't offer you anything more than I could offer Sarah. I can make love to you, I can provide for you——'

'But you can't give your time and your heart?' she offered quietly.

He didn't say a word, not one, just held her eyes tenderly. She didn't understand him; how could he be so certain of that? A challenge stirred inside her, a very odd one. Did she have a chance of persuading him otherwise? That it was possible for him to love and give his time and his heart? And was that what she truly wanted? Those thoughts frightened her.

'I think we'd better eat before the food spoils,' she suggested, and turned away from him.

'Verity?'

She turned.

'It doesn't end here, you know,' he told her bluntly.

She nodded and this time knew the truth when it was put to her. She said after only a moment's consideration, 'I know. It's only the beginning.'

CHAPTER SIX

HER body burned. Verity flung the bedclothes from her and sat up. The bedroom was cool but she burned, an inward heat that pulsed through her.

They had talked all evening. The spaghetti had been good and the wine heady and she had fully expected Rupert to try to make love to her in front of the fire.

But he hadn't and she knew why. It had been an evening of exorcism. They had talked about their ex-lovers as if they needed to clear a path through their emotions before taking their own course.

Now she burned. She held her head in her hands. She burned with need, the need for Rupert Scott to hold and love her.

'Verity?'

Her hand shot to the bedside lamp and she snapped it on.

'Can't you sleep?' he asked in little more than a husky whisper. He stood in the doorway, wrapped in a white towelling robe. His hair was damp as if he'd just stepped from the shower. Verity glanced at her travelling clock.

'It's three o'clock. What are you doing up?'

He stepped into the room. 'I've been working. Come, I want to show you something.'

Verity scrambled out of bed and slid into her satin robe. He took her to his bedroom and she fully expected his computer to be glaring and the final page of his screenplay displayed to be read.

'What?'

He slid his arm around her shoulders and led her to the window. A full moon hung moodily in the black sky, and Verity exhaled a small gasp at the huge moonbow that caressed it.

'They say it's a sign of rain,' he murmured behind her and slid his arms down and around her waist. She felt his warm breath on the top of her head and his heart pulsing in her back.

This was the beginning and she was ready for it. The end she didn't even want to try to foresee. It was the moment, the time. She leaned back into him and clasped her hands across his. 'I didn't think you were romantic,' she murmured. The heat was already building up inside her, the heat and need that had woken her.

'There's a lot you don't know about me and a lot you're going to find out very shortly.'

He turned her into his arms and she went willingly, her mouth seeking his as urgently as he sought hers. The kiss was wild and frenetic, as if the world had only minutes to live its last. Verity coiled her fingers into his damp hair, almost clawed at him with the passion that rose so desperately inside her. Rupert ran his hands down her back, pressing his thumbs into her hips and grinding her against him.

Suddenly he lifted her and lay her down on his bed.

'I think you arranged that moon just to get me into your room,' she murmured as he lay beside her, gathering her into his arms to hold her against his body.

'I can't make love to you in a single bed.'

'So you're not romantic after all,' she laughed softly into his cheek.

'I arranged the moon for you, didn't I?'

She didn't answer because her mouth was too busy, grazing across his jawline, seeking his mouth once again.

He groaned under the pressure and then he parted her lips and explored the soft silkiness of her inner lips with his tongue. Verity's heart and senses spun with the depth of her passion for him. She slid her hand into his robe and smoothed her fingers over his chest, caressing the hair and the muscled flesh beneath.

His exploration was equally heated. He pushed her robe aside and smoothed her nightie up over her thighs and then lowered his head to kiss the smooth planes of her stomach. Verity arched against him, feverishly pulling at his robe to completely release his body from any confinement.

At last she felt his heated flesh on hers and, drugged with the intoxication of it, she gasped out his name and rushed her hands down over his hips.

She marvelled at the sheer splendour and power of his body. It was taut and power-packed, hot and hard, yet yielding under her every caress.

He lowered his head and drew on her creamy breasts as her hands made contact with his arousal. The power that charged through them both was catastrophic. Verity cried out and he steadied her with his mouth, desperately trying to cool the heat with small, soothing kisses on her face and neck that did little but heighten her need to the point of explosion.

His legs entwined with hers as he crushed her to him, moving restlessly, urgently against her perfumed flesh. And then his mouth crushed hers once again, his tongue fierce in its deep exploration.

There was just one small tremor of his hand as he parted her thighs, as if even now he was unsure of her. With a single smooth, elongated caress of his arousal Verity soothed his uncertainty and, gauging her need, his fingers parted her silky womanhood and began his seductive prelude.

Oh, God, he was beautiful, his tantalising thrusts so skilled and sensuous. Her orgasm rose and hovered and hung suspended in the web of her ecstasy. She desperately wanted to please him before wallowing in her own pleasure but her caresses weren't enough. She wanted to give every part of herself, to give him everything. Her most intimate love.

'Dear God, Verity,' he moaned. 'Don't do that.'

She did. Unashamedly she lowered her head and kissed him tenderly, caressed him with her tongue and lips, drew deeply on his lust till he shuddered deeply with the intimate pleasure she was giving him. And then he would allow her no more but lifted her away from him and rolled her over.

He entered her immediately, his breathing heavy and harsh. And she was ready for him, curling her arms around him possessively and drawing him deeply into her suppliant body. They moved awkwardly for a fraction of a second, but then the rhythm was set and their urgency unleashed as they rose higher and higher into that red vortex of liquid pleasure and hedonism.

Verity cried out as she came and then cried again as his orgasm swelled inside her. He let out a shuddering groan, so deep and primeval that her heart raced excitedly at the power she had over him at that moment. But she didn't feel triumph at that power, more a pride and a fantastic thrill that she had excited him so deeply.

They lay in each other's arms for a long while before raising the strength to speak. And when they did they spoke soft intimate praises to each other.

They slept at last and, when Verity awoke in the morning, Rupert was still there, coiled into her back, holding her as if never to let her go.

And so it began. The affair she had fought against and lost and didn't regret for a minute.

Verity loaded the washing-machine and stood back, watching her underwear tumbling with his, and smiled.

'What are you grinning at?' Rupert came up behind her and slid his arms around her waist.

'That.' She grinned happily, and nodded at the machine. 'Our washing, sloshing around so intimately.'

'Hmm. What's it supposed to mean?'

Verity shrugged. To her it meant everything. That very special closeness, somehow more intimate than anything else they shared, apart from bed, of course. It might be an imperfect affair but their lovemaking was perfect enough.

'It's a woman's thing that men wouldn't understand,' she murmured, leaning her head back so he could graze his lips down the side of her face.

'I'll leave it alone, then,' he laughed, and spun her round and kissed her lips. When they parted he flicked her hair behind her ears. 'I'm going to the village—what do we need?'

He'd got into the habit of going to the village most mornings and he never offered to take her, not that she wanted to go. She had far too much to do. They'd slid into a very domestic routine. While Rupert shopped she did the housework. They lunched together, mostly outside on the sunny terrace, as the weather had turned so good, and then parted company for the afternoon to work. Though that didn't always pan out. Sometimes Rupert would come to her room and they would make love, unhurriedly, as if they were on a permanent honeymoon and had all the time in the world to indulge themselves.

Verity moved away from him and picked up a pencil and paper and made a list. When he'd gone she stood staring at the washing-machine. It was all so unreal. This old mill house, her love for Rupert Scott, his insatiable appetite for her.

She loved him, had known it for days now, but deep in her aching heart she sensed he didn't love her. He made love to her beautifully, sometimes very erotically, anywhere he pleased and always satisfactorily, but there was never any talk about their feelings for each other or of their future or what would happen when they both had to return to England.

Sometimes she suspected he called Sarah from the village because when he came back he was quiet and morose, and sometimes she suspected he was thinking of her when he was making love to her.

She wished she didn't have these suspicions because they were without foundation, but they were there nevertheless and added to her insecurity.

'I've brought you a present.'

In surprise Verity turned to him from the computer. He tossed her a plastic bag.

'Market-ware, but it comes from the heart.' He grinned as she pulled the garish T-shirt from the bag.

'I don't believe it!' she screeched. 'It's perfectly hid...' She stopped and bit her lip. Perhaps he thought it was fantastic. It was huge, bright red with a lurid appliquéd parrot on the front. It sparkled with gold and silver sequins, not her style at all.

'It's a bit of fun, Verity,' Rupert assured her, noting the look of horror on her face.

Verity smiled up at him, but there was a deep sadness in her heart. Yes, it was a bit of fun, but the parrot reminded her of her remark about her cousin and her boss being sick as parrots if their plan didn't work. Part of it had worked. She had fallen in love with Rupert and that was the only part, nothing else. The T-shirt was also a painful reminder that their time together was nearly up. Another week and it would all be over.

'It's lovely,' Verity croaked. 'No, I mean it.' Her eyes twinkled mischievously. 'It's just what I need to clean out the bath.'

He was upon her in a second, laughing and sweeping her up into his arms and crushing him to her.

'For that, you'll wear it as a penance,' and he added throatily, 'now.'

'You want me to actually *wear* it?' she giggled.

And when he held her away from him she knew the look in his eyes and her heart hammered out her acceptance.

'Turn your back,' she murmured coyly and he did, with a smile of resignation.

'OK,' she said. 'You can look now.'

It was made for an Amazon and hung limply from her narrow shoulders and skimmed her thighs. But he looked at her as if she were swathed in the most sensuous of eastern silks, his grey, moody eyes eating her hungrily.

He held his hands out to her and she stepped into his embrace and buried her face in his sweater so he wouldn't see the tears in her eyes. His arms enfolded her and held her tightly and then he lowered his mouth to hers, crushing her lips so desperately that she stemmed a cry of pain.

Their lovemaking was different this time. He insisted she keep the T-shirt on; he thought it sexy and arousing and slid his hands under it to caress and arouse her. For Verity it was heartbreaking. She quickly went under his spell but her heart ached at all the gift meant to her. Losing him, having to face Stuart and Alan. It was a life she didn't want any more. She wanted Rupert's life, not his working empire and that fifteen-roomed house with the lingering perfume of his ex-mistress, but this life, eating and working together and sprawling in front of the olive-wood fire at the end of the day.

She blotted it all away as Rupert made love to her, feverishly, as if he too was aware of the time slipping away from them. His thrusts were deep and penetrating, his kisses executed with that same urgency, and when at last there was no more energy and strength left they allowed their orgasm to swell and burst till there was nothing left but their hot breath, their skin raw and aching, their muted kisses and weak caresses fading as the afternoon sun faded over the distant hill.

Later they cooked a meal together and tried to recapture something of their passion over the last few days. But something had changed, and neither knew what it was, and neither spoke of it.

'Did you manage to finish it?' Rupert asked.

Verity was exhausted. Time had been running out, but the book was finished now. She peered into the casserole Rupert was stirring on the kitchen table.

'Yes, and I can't say I'm sorry.' She poured two glasses of wine and sat down while Rupert dished up the food. 'Towards the end I was beginning to think the whole idea of the wedding book a waste of time and effort. Thank goodness it's fact not fiction. It must be awful to be writing something you haven't any heart for. It must show.'

'I'm sure it'll be a success, though. The bride-to-be market must be quite a lucrative one. And, talking of weddings...'

Verity held her breath and her heart stilled. She watched his eyes, searching, searching.

'...how would you like to go to one?'

Her heart, already overworked and flagging, began to pulse feebly. 'Whose?' she murmured, trying to keep the hope out of her voice.

'The guy who owns the bar in the village. He's getting married tomorrow and has invited us both.'

'He doesn't know me!' Verity protested. Her heart was back to normal and so were her wits. Had she really expected a proposal?

'The whole village is invited. Shall we go?'

She didn't want to, absolutely not. It would be painful. But she wanted to get out of the old mill house. Apart from a few walks when the weather had been good, they had never ventured out together. They'd been cocooned for almost a month, living and loving together and not seeing another living soul. Perhaps too much of a good thing.

'Why not?' she answered coolly.

The wedding-day dawned bright and beautiful. Verity lay next to Rupert, her arm across his chest, and gazed out of the window. Their last full day together and they were going to a wedding. Her heart ached for it to be their own, but that was a hopeless dream. Yet she would settle for just one declaration of love from Rupert. She didn't need marriage but she needed him in her life to love her; perhaps that was a hopeless dream too.

They had their breakfast on the terrace, laughing and joking, but there was a void already opening up between them, stilting that humour.

'When will you be coming back to England?' she asked him as she sat back and sipped her coffee. The sky was so blue it made her ache inside. There was the sweet scent of pine in the air and she wanted to remember this forever.

'I don't know, maybe next week. I'll see how I survive without you.' He was grinning as he said it and for once Verity didn't appreciate the smile.

'You'll have to make your own bed and do your own washing-up from now on.' She kept her voice light. She didn't want him to know how desperate she felt about leaving.

'I managed before.' This time there was no accompanying grin.

And you'll manage without me forever because there isn't anything there, Verity mournfully thought. He'd made it clear from the start that he wasn't promising anything, and if she had fallen in love with him she only had herself to blame. She had been warned.

'We'd better get ready,' she said brightly and stood up to clear the dishes. Rupert was still sitting there after she had washed up, distant and morose and gazing into space.

The village church was packed and cold, and Rupert slid his arm around her to keep her warm.

'The bride is quite fat,' Rupert whispered, 'she obviously hasn't read your book.'

'It wouldn't have done her much good—she's pregnant!'

They discussed this on their way home, after the reception, which was held in the local bar and spilled out on to the plaza. Rupert drove and Verity sat next to him, clutching a piece of the bridegroom's tie in her hand. At the reception the groom's tie had been cut into small pieces and each guest had bought a piece, and the money collected was part of the couple's dowry. Verity was enthralled by the custom, amazed how sensible and practical it was.

'Must have been a shotgun wedding,' was Rupert's cynical contribution to the discussion.

'Not necessarily,' Verity argued. 'They were obviously very much in love.'

'They had no choice but to put a brave face on. An abortion in a Catholic village like this was probably out of the question.'

'The question probably didn't even arise!' Verity snapped back. 'They were in love and wanted that child; their timing was just a bit out, that's all. Why do men always think abortion is the answer?'

'I didn't say that, Verity,' Rupert insisted darkly as they turned into the pink driveway.

'OK, let's drop it,' she suggested flintily, and was the first out of the car and into the house.

She left Rupert to lay the fire and ran upstairs to her bedroom to change her clothes. It had been a long day and she was tired and her suitcase was staring at her as she opened her bedroom door. Oh, God, this was their last night together. She slumped down on to the bed and held her head in her hands.

How would they leave it? Would he want to see her in England? It would be different in England. Both returning to such a very different life from the one they had shared here.

'I'll drive you to the airport tomorrow,' he told her when she came downstairs. So their parting had been on his mind too.

'It's not necessary,' she told him quietly as she passed him to go to the kitchen.

He caught her wrist and pulled her to him, but not into his arms, just in front of him so he could pressure her shoulders and keep her still.

'It is necessary,' he insisted. 'It's a long drive and . . .'

'And you'll have to get a taxi back——'

'It isn't a problem.'

'I don't *want* you to drive me to the airport!' Her voice rose dramatically and she swallowed hard. 'I'd much rather go on my own,' she said more levelly.

'Do you hate airport goodbyes?'

Her heart iced. And it would be goodbye. He'd said it and he meant it.

'They don't bother me,' she told him dismissively and tried to shift away from him.

It seemed to irritate him and his fingers tightened on her shoulders.

'I warned you, Verity. I warned you I couldn't make any promises——'

'About what?' she stormed, angry now because of her disappointment. 'Us? I knew the score, Rupert. I don't expect anything from you, so don't waste your breath offering me excuses.'

'I'm offering you nothing of the sort. I didn't want any of this to happen——'

'But it did, and whatever you say it won't right a wrong.'

'It was wrong, was it?'

He obviously didn't think it had been, but then he wasn't suffering and she wasn't going to show him she was.

'No, it wasn't,' she offered on a sigh. She looked into his eyes but they were as unreadable as when first they had met. For a short time, since she had loved him, she had seen those eyes soften, but no more. 'I have no regrets, Rupert, but tomorrow I go home and I have a life and a job to pick up on and that's all I need.'

His fingers bit into her fiercely. 'That's all you've ever needed, isn't it? Someone to ease your way back into life after Mike's death.'

'Well, we did each other a favour, didn't we?'

'Meaning?'

'You filled a few gaps in my life and I filled a few in yours. We're quits, so let's leave the score even, shall we?'

'So this was all a game to you——'

'Some game, some damned rules! You started all this, Rupert,' she cried. 'If you had just kept yourself to yourself, just as we had arranged——'

'Stop it, Verity,' he growled. 'You sound like one of those typical females I despise so much.'

'Oh, the Sarah sort? You know, I can sympathise with her. Life with you must have been a miserable tirade. I bet the poor girl didn't know where she was with you from one day to the next.'

He said nothing but his eyes darkened so threateningly that she felt fear rattle its chains. She pulled herself away from him and rubbed her shoulders.

'I'm sorry——'

'Don't apologise for the truth,' he rasped. 'Sarah too was quite inept at voicing her opinions till she walked out on me. Now she just sends me bills, but I don't fall into those traps so easily now——'

'How dare you? How dare you insinuate that I would do the same?'

'I didn't. You took it that way. Now listen, Verity,' he ordered blackly, 'I told you from the off that I'm not into the wedded-bliss game——'

'Who mentioned marriage?' she stormed, her eyes wide and raging.

'No one, but before you get any ideas——'

'I haven't any ideas, Rupert bloody Scott. And that is your big problem. You think that every female that comes on to you wants marriage. So Sarah gave you a hard time—tough. I won't. I've enjoyed our affair but if I never saw you again it would be too soon!'

She swung from him then and powered out to the kitchen. She wanted to power up to her bedroom but that would show she cared and was ready for a good sulk. Well, she'd get on with the dinner and just show him she didn't care a damn about leaving him tomorrow.

Later, when they were in bed and making love for the last time, Verity behaved badly. She knew what she was doing and her only excuse was that she was hurting so badly inside that it seemed the only way. She was demanding; not verbally, she didn't have to speak; her hungry body said it all. But at the same time she gave as good as she demanded, wanting to store away every caress, every kiss, every hungry thrust of his manhood in her memory banks.

Deep into the night when he slept beside her she coiled herself into him and cried quietly to herself, ashamed and remorseful for demanding so much of him. She smoothed her hands over his exhausted body and kissed his lips softly and let her tears dry on his face. It was all she had to leave him, tears of sorrow and regret for their very imperfect affair.

CHAPTER SEVEN

'HAVE you got everything?'

How banal, how damned unoriginal! Verity wanted to scream it but didn't. It would show her bitterness and Rupert would read it as sadness, and she had her pride.

'Yes, everything,' she told him brightly.

He settled her lap-top computer on the back seat of the hired car and slammed shut the door.

'I can still drive you down to the airport.'

'Forget it,' Verity told him with a forced smile. 'It's a lovely day. I'll enjoy it better on my own.'

She thought she saw hurt in his eyes but she had thought she'd seen much more this morning when he had woken her with soft tempting kisses. But she was wrong, of course, just hopefully seeking something that wasn't there.

'I'll phone you,' he murmured as he took her in his arms for the last time.

'Yes, that would be nice,' she murmured back and as his mouth closed over hers she wondered how he would do that, for he didn't know her number or where she lived or very much about her at all. She wondered that because she was forcing herself to think of anything but what was really on her mind—the terrible feeling of loss.

She didn't look back, not even a glance in the rear-view mirror, not even a perfunctory wave out of the open window as she rattled down the dirt-track road and out of his life.

'Who sent the roses?' Alan asked a few weeks later. They'd arrived that morning. Delivered to the office because that was the only place he knew where to find her.

'A secret admirer, probably,' Verity told him and nothing more. The card with no message, simply Rupert's name on it, was ripped and in the bin. If only he'd written something . . .

'A bit late for Valentine's Day.'

'Is it?'

Verity didn't even bother to look up from her work. She was still frosty with Alan. On her first day back to work she had coldly told him exactly what she thought of him, as she had done her cousin Stuart. She had also told them that absolutely nothing had come of their disgusting plan and she didn't want to hear another word mentioned about Rupert Scott. The subject was closed.

'Still mad with us?' Alan asked quietly, determined to reopen it. He sounded repentant and Verity wavered.

She looked up then. They would never know how much. She was mad with everyone, even herself. How could she have been so stupid and let all this happen? Now she was going to pay for that disastrous affair, more than she could ever have anticipated.

'I feel sorry for you both more than anything, not that you deserve my sympathy,' she retored loftily. 'You and your warped ambition, willing to sacrifice my honour for your own ends, and as for

Stuart, poor soul, my heart bleeds for him, he's getting his come-uppance all right, at the hands of his greedy grabbing wife, your sister Angie.'

'It was her idea, you know,' Alan told her, ignoring the slur on his sister and perching on her desk as if ready for a good old heart-to-heart.

Verity shuffled papers. She really didn't need this. She sighed. 'I'm not surprised by anything that Angie does, but what does surprise me is the way you both went along with it. I really believed you cared about me.'

'We do, and we thought we were helping.'

'Helping yourself!' Verity cried. Her hand came up and kneaded her feverish brow. She didn't feel well and hadn't felt well since she had realised ...

'That was an afterthought.'

Verity's eyes widened. 'An afterthought?'

'It was true that Stuart arranged that dinner party to get you two together, thinking that it might help you and us, but the rest was all to do with Angie.'

'Yes, I can imagine! You two amaze me, grown men as well, manipulated by little Angie,' she gibed sarcastically.

'She didn't manipulate us, Verity,' Alan said calmly, 'just made us see something we missed. She saw the look in Rupert Scott's eyes every time he looked at you.'

'Oh, yes.' Verity smiled cynically. She didn't believe the look could have been anything but derisive. 'Contempt, was it?'

'Far from it,' Alan smiled. 'Women are far more astute than us poor blind males. Angie saw the interest, the attraction, the lust, if you like.'

Verity shook her head in disbelief. 'Rubbish. Shall I tell you something? He didn't even remember my name when I turned up at El Molino. Hardly the reaction you'd expect from a man champing at the bit. No, Angie saw what she'd hoped to see, Alan. She *wanted* Rupert to be interested in me, for her own ends!'

Why, she'd done the very same thing herself. Imagined that Rupert had cared for her when she had caught him looking at her in a certain way. But looks were deceptive and, besides, they weren't enough, nor were bouquets of red roses with no message!

'That's unfair, Verity. We all care very deeply for you. Do you honestly believe we would have arranged for the pair of you to spend such an intimate time together if we didn't think some sort of happiness for you would come out of it?'

Verity lost her temper then. She stood up and angrily faced her boss. 'You wanted to get us together for his advertising and his magazines——'

'OK, what we did was out of order but worse things have been done in the name of business; nevertheless, we all hoped you would get some happiness out of it,' Alan insisted.

'Well, I didn't!' Verity cried, trying to hide the hurt from him. The opposite, the very opposite. Even the good times had soured now. How could she have even thought she'd been happy in that old mill house when her love hadn't been returned?

'I'm sorry about that,' Alan offered at last after studying her intently. 'But I know it all looks black to you and our intentions not particularly honourable, but when Angie saw the way he looked at you...well...we just thought no harm would be done.'

No harm done, she mused ironically after Alan had left. If only they all knew how deeply the damage went. She stared at the deep red roses. Moonlight and roses, she had never thought it possible from him. And if only this hadn't happened...her hand strayed to her stomach...she could appreciate that he might, he just might care a tiny bit. But she had to force herself to think otherwise, that the moonlight had been a prelude to the affair and the roses the grand finale.

'I...I didn't expect you so early.'

Verity stood back from the door of her first-floor flat. Her heart was pounding erratically but Rupert stood as still as a statue in front of her. The Rupert Scott she had first known; sophisticated, cool and aloof. She knew then that Angie had been very wrong and hadn't seen any sign of interest in those cool grey eyes. They weren't capable of showing or feeling *any* emotion.

'Aren't you going to ask me in?' were his first stiff words.

She stood back further and let him step into the small hallway. He turned to her as she closed the door after him.

'Why the coolness on the phone, Verity?'

She led him through to her small sitting-room. She'd made it as comfortable as possible for him, lit the gas log fire, bought fresh flowers that very morning, plumped up the cushions. She wanted to show him that she had a life without him and a pleasant one too.

'I was just surprised you'd called. How did you know my telephone number?'

'Don't be absurd. I looked in the telephone book, of course.' His voice was brittle.

Of course. She hadn't thought. The call and his request to see her had been such a surprise that she hadn't wondered till now how he had known her number.

'Sit down,' she offered nervously.

He did, in her favourite armchair. He looked so very different from the Rupert she had loved in Andalucia. His hair had been cut since then and was stylishly blow-dried. He looked good in his formal grey suit, almost the same colour as his eyes. She still loved him; how could she stop?

'Did you get the flowers?'

'Yes, thank you.'

There was a long, long silence in which Rupert stared at the floor and Verity watched him staring at the floor. They had shared so much and now suddenly there was an unbridgeable gulf between them.

'The cold farewell at El Molino, the frosty phone call, and now this bleak reception,' he said at last. 'Are you trying to tell me something, Verity?' He looked up at her then, his jawline stretched taut as if he was gritting his teeth.

Verity stood by the fire, leaning one arm on the stripped-pine mantelpiece. She felt at an advantage standing and she needed to be at an advantage with him, but all the same her insides twisted painfully.

'It depends on what you want to hear,' she said coldly.

Another awkward silence before he spoke. 'When you left El Molino so breezily I hoped you were just putting on a brave face. I'd like to believe you didn't give me a backward glance because your eyes were filled with tears.'

She couldn't believe his cruelty. Had he come here to turn the knife? 'I...I can't believe we are discussing something so very unimportant——'

He stood up suddenly, taking her by surprise and grasping her arm. 'Well, it is important, damned important. I want to know what's going on in that unemotional mind of yours. Tell me, Verity, were you crying?'

'The hell I was!' she snapped sarcastically. 'I had my eyes on that dirt track and there were no tears in them, I assure you!' She shook his hand from her arm. Why was he doing this to her, rubbing her face in the mud? 'Why did you bother phoning, Rupert, why did you bother coming here?'

'Because I thought we had something going——'

'Something going,' she echoed. Suddenly she understood and she had to fight back the tears and the pain. He was here because he *did* care, but the timing, just like that of the loving bride and groom in Andalucia, was way out. Oh, God, if only...

'We had an affair,' she cut in, 'a very imperfect affair.' She laced her voice with contempt because that was the way it had to be. 'And I can't see it going any further.'

'I told you in Spain that I wasn't in a position to offer you anything more.'

'I'm not asking for anything more, Rupert. I never have done. But I don't want it to go on.' How it tore at her heart to say that. 'Andalucia was... well, it was different...'

'A holiday romance?' he blazed contemptuously.

'Hardly a holiday,' she spluttered. 'We were both working our socks off.'

'In and out of bed.'

Verity flushed. 'Don't bring it down to that level,' she breathed huskily.

'Gutter-level? You brought it down, Verity, by your dismissive attitude on that last day. As if you'd had your fun and it was over and you were quite happy to be going home...' He stopped, unable to go on, and Verity gazed at him in dismay.

How could he think that? How could he? Surely he must have known how badly she was hurting and that she was putting on a front to hide her hurt? If only he had said he loved her and wanted to see her back in England because he couldn't live without her. But he hadn't, and now it was too late. Minutes ago she had thought he might care, but all he'd come for was to ressurrect that Spanish affair.

Verity braced herself to be hard and resolute. 'In that case, why suggest I might have been crying as I left? A bit of a contradiction... Look, this is getting us nowhere,' she breathed sensibly. 'Now, why are you here? To say that maybe we had something going——'

'I came here to talk to you, over dinner—out, not in——'

'I don't want to go out——'

'Well, out it's going to be,' he rasped thickly, 'because if we stay here a minute longer I'm going to take you to bed and positively remind you of just what we had going in Andalucia.' His eyes were smoked dark grey as he issued that warning and Verity didn't doubt he would do just that.

'Sex,' Verity hissed in harsh defence, 'that's what we had, Rupert, and a lot of it. Too much, because now there isn't any more left.'

'So damned sure of that, are you?' He lifted her chin with burning fingers and lowered his lips to hers. Not in a gesture of love or even passion but a gesture of punishment and revenge and to prove a point.

Verity tore her mouth away, shocked at how cold and unfeeling she could be. But she had to be because now there was no hope. Later would come the remorse and more suffering because he was trying, and she recognised that even if he wasn't offering her some sort of permanency in their relationship... he nevertheless wanted it to continue. But she couldn't, not now that she was... was carrying his child. Because at some stage he would have to know and the trap would close around them both.

His burning fingers cooled and he grazed them over her jaw. His eyes softened and Verity felt her strength dangerously weaken. Don't let him say something nice, she prayed.

'Verity. Things have changed since Spain. I'm freer now to offer——'

'I don't want anything,' she interrupted painfully. Oh, she did, she wanted it all, his life and love twinned with hers. But now there was a barrier between them that neither of them could have dreamed of.

'I can't believe that,' he breathed and his lips came to hers again, and this time there was no anger but for Verity the punishment was worse. His mouth was warm and sensuous, pleading, demanding, seeking her submission.

And she felt her resolution slipping from her and she was blindly clawing in the dark for something to hold on to.

'Rupert,' she implored when he eased his lips from hers. She had to try to stop this. 'You . . . you wanted to talk . . . so tell me . . . what do you mean, freer?'

It had heatedly crossed her mind that he might have lied about his relationship with Sarah and that they had been married and perhaps now a divorce was imminent. But what difference, what difference?

He held her gently in his arms now, confident that he had broken down her reserve. 'I've sorted out a few things in my life and my mind,' he whispered against her pale blonde hair. 'I want you to come and live with me, Verity.'

She pulled away from him slightly to look into his face. Her eyes were violet orbs of surprise. 'Live with you?' she husked. She hadn't expected that, not at all.

He smiled and smoothed a wisp of hair from her temple. 'Don't sound so aghast, it's not a sin, and you said——'

'Yes, I said, didn't I?' she murmured, remembering and regretting it now. If two people cared about each other, why not live together? But now she was in love and feeling very different. Surely marriage, that definite, wonderful commitment, was the only way. But Rupert didn't love her because if he did he would want that as much as she did. But he did want her by his side, so surely that was a caring start? But now, how wrong the timing.

'I . . . I don't think that's a very good idea.' She lowered her eyes so he couldn't see her pain.

'Why? It's no different from us living together in the old mill house.'

Couldn't he see that it was? She shook her head and he stilled it with his hands clasped each side of her face. He tilted her face up. 'Don't argue with me, Verity,' he said earnestly. 'It's what I want and I believe it's what you want.'

Her lashes flickered over her eyes and she bit her lip. 'I don't think you're ready for another relationship so soon after Sarah,' she husked.

He laughed softly. 'That's my affair and not your problem.'

'But . . . but it is,' Verity insisted. All her insecurities flew to the defence of her aching emotions. Sarah, bloody Sarah; he claimed he was free of her but she couldn't accept that he was. There was something blocking it for her but she didn't know what.

Rupert's eyes darkened. 'It isn't, Verity. Leave it alone. It's history, so forget it. I don't keep harping on about your affair with Mike, do I?'

'Mike is dead and no threat; Sarah is alive, and you know that's different.'

He sighed deeply, slightly edgily. 'And it always will be in your eyes. Forget it, Verity, forget them. I want you with me and I want to provide for you——'

'And you want to make love to me every night?'

He missed the aggrieved tone in her voice and gathered her into his arms again. His charisma and sensuality overpowered her as his mouth crushed hers, parting her lips with the insistence of his probing tongue, giving her his answer in the impassioned kiss.

She felt it all slip out of her grasp, the fight, the reasoning she had thought she had already coped with. How easy to love him, how easy to let him have his way and go and live with him in the hope that he might learn to love her, not just care for her. But the... the baby? So very wrong and out of place in this relationship that was already so unstable.

His hands slid under her silk shirt and her breasts were ready for him. Engorged and heated and so desperate for his touch. He moaned passionately against her throat and trailed searing kisses down to the opening of her shirt. Easily he released the small pearl buttons and then, so easily and swiftly, he lowered his head to draw from her nipples every last vestige of rebellion.

She clawed at his hair, closed her eyes and threw her head back to let out a silent mouthed moan of submission. He had such power, such demanding insatiable power over her, and she couldn't fight it and in that moment didn't want to. Already his hands were at the zipper of her jeans and her hand came down and helped him.

Their clothes were discarded with almost indecent rapidity and Rupert with one deep persuasive kiss lowered her to the rug in front of the fire. He straddled her, gently and tenderly caressing her breast and watching the flush of desire rise and deepen the colour of her cheeks.

'You feel different,' he murmured throatily.

Surely he couldn't have noticed the subtle difference in her body? It was only weeks, not months. The pain of having to tell him knifed through her. But not now, she couldn't tell him now.

'Do I feel different?' he asked and there was no mistaking the suggestion in his tone.

She gave herself to him then, smiled up at him and lifted her hands to caress him. As she stroked and smoothed his beautiful muscled arousal she blanked off everything but the pleasure of giving and receiving. She loved him so very much and for the time being it was enough that he wanted her so strongly and passionately.

His first thrust was tentative, as if afraid to hurt her, as if he knew that a tiny life was blossoming inside her, but he couldn't know, of course. His life, she mouthed to herself as she urged against him, her body telling him in its frenzy that she wanted him so very deeply inside her. She smoothed his hips and pulled him into her and he responded with such passion that she was suddenly afraid. And then there was no more fear but the dizzy need that couldn't be held back any longer. Harder and faster and somehow more penetrating than their love-making before, and then that last desperate sprint in case that miraculous feeling slipped out of reach and Rupert steadying her, gripping her hips in that last shuddering penetration as their orgasm spun their hearts and their bodies through space and time.

Later his kisses soothed her wet brow and his fingers teased the moist silken flesh of her inner thighs.

'You *do* feel different,' he whispered.

She wondered at the heightened awareness of her body. Every sense and nerve pulse seemed crazily near the surface of her skin. Was it because of that tiny bud of life forming deeply within her? Or was it that she had missed him so desperately?

Rupert moved his hand higher and she felt the heat rise so rapidly that even he was surprised. He laughed, softly against her breast, and as his hand started a pulsing rhythm between her legs his mouth closed over her nipple and in the instant he drew on it Verity arched her back and cried out.

Minutes later she was still trembling in his arms, shocked at the intensity of what had just happened.

'I don't know what came over me,' she whispered.

'Whatever, I'm glad.' He leaned on one elbow and gazed down at her. 'You have an incredible sexuality.'

Verity blushed. 'Don't you mean insatiability?' She was embarrassed now.

'That as well,' he murmured. 'Parting obviously makes the heart grow fonder.'

'Or needier,' she responded cryptically, and tried to get up from the rug.

Rupert pulled her back and his voice was harsh when he spoke. 'I didn't like that remark——'

'I didn't like you making me come like that!'

'For God's sake, Verity, what's got into you? We've never been this way before.'

She sat up and buried her head in her knees. 'I...I don't understand.' She really didn't. They had been so close and uninhibited before, but now... 'I...I don't like the power you have over me.'

'What power, for heaven's sake?' He tried to prise her head from her knees but she wouldn't let him. 'Verity,' he tried to soothe, 'we know each other well enough not be shy with each other.'

'Sexually, you mean?' She raised her head and looked at him. 'It seems this relationship is all about sex. OK, so we're good together in bed or on the floor or wherever, but is it good enough for us to live together? You came here tonight with all your demands off pat, but what about me?'

'What about you?' he asked incredulously.

'Yeah, what about me?' she drawled sarcastically. She struggled up and reached down for her shirt and slid it round her shoulders. 'You demand too much, Rupert, you expect too much. *You* insist I go and live with you; well, perhaps I don't want to. Perhaps I want——'

'Marriage?' he rasped bitterly.

Oh, no, suddenly this wasn't about marriage. It was about loving and caring, and Rupert Scott had shown none of that. But by the very mention of marriage he must assume that she loved him enough to want that. Well, she wouldn't let him have the satisfaction of knowing she cared that deeply for him.

'I don't care a mouldy fig for marriage.' Her eyes were very vivid when she added with a challenge, 'You want me to live with you? OK, I will, but I live my own life——'

'Don't start bargaining with me!'

'No bargaining, Rupert, take it or leave it, I'll live with you but I go my own way and I don't mean with men. I mean with my career and what I do with it, and my time. Yes, my time——'

'Forget it, then,' he slammed back brutally. He got up and started to throw his clothes on, far more determinedly than he had discarded them. 'I want you in my life but I don't want a repeat of what I've been through before—life with conditions.'

'You wouldn't get it because I'm not the jealous, possessive type. I wouldn't grizzle if you stayed out all night. I wouldn't be another Sarah in your life,' she flamed. She would, though; she was lying through her teeth, because she'd be exactly like Sarah, wanting him to spend time with her, hating every minute he was out of her life.

'I repeat, forget it. I've just got rid of one helluva bitch and I don't need another!'

Verity realised she had been backtracking with her last remark. Dizzily she rubbed at her forehead. She didn't know what she was doing or saying any more. She'd actually agreed to go and live with him and she didn't know why she'd said it. Desperation perhaps. Suddenly her head cleared.

'Wait, Rupert,' she murmured as he slid into his suit jacket and turned away as if to leave.

He stopped and looked at her warily.

'Let me make some coffee and let's talk some more.' Suddenly she desperately wanted him to stay. She *did* want to talk. She wanted to find out what he truly wanted and if there was a remote chance of making something of this crazy relationship.

'You mean bargain some more?' His mouth twisted wryly. 'No sale, Verity. I've made my offer and *you* take it or leave it.'

What was the use? It was all one way with him, his way. 'You selfish bastard!' she grazed spitefully at him.

'Substitute bitch for bastard and you have a perfect description of yourself,' he retorted with deathly calm. 'You're up and down like a Yo-Yo and I'm not even going to question what you really want, Verity, because I don't think you know yourself——'

'But I know what you want, Rupert,' she flamed back. 'You want what you came here for tonight, sex on demand, and to make it easier for yourself you want me on an intravenous drip in your own house so you don't even have to go out for it——'

She thought he was going to be the first man to strike her. Her head reeled as he crunched her shoulders up round her ears.

'What the hell has got into you since you got back from Andalucia? You're different, a rotten little spoiled brat!'

'And what are you but a spoiled brat too?' she cried. 'All I hear from you is self, self, self. My life isn't a consideration. I said if I came to live with you I'd want my own life, but you're not even willing to...' Her voice trailed away on a sea of realisation. It swirled around her, spinning her crazily. She had made it clear to him that she wanted a life but he didn't want her to have one. Love or mere possessiveness? There could be a thin line between the two or a yawning gap. She didn't know which, but if she lived with him she would surely find out. Did she want to go that far?

Oh, God, she did. She loved him and she was desperate for him to love her, so she had to give him a chance but . . . but there was so much that frightened her. She didn't want to be another Sarah.

'Rupert,' she went on, and because her voice wasn't so shrill he eased the pressure on her shoulders. 'I have to say this and please don't tell me to forget it. It's something I need to know . . .'

'Dear God, not Sarah again?' His eyes were black with suppressed fury but suddenly they softened. 'Look, get it out of your system because it's obviously blocking your reasoning.'

'It isn't,' she insisted and then bit her lip because she knew it was. 'It's nothing major. But you said . . . you implied tonight that you'd just got rid of her and I . . . I thought you'd said she'd left six months before.'

His grip turned to a gentle caress. 'Darling, she did. I didn't lie to you and it's what I meant when I said I was freer now, freer to offer you more. Since Sarah left I've been maintaining her, paying her bills . . .'

'Guilt money?' Verity ventured in a tight whisper.

He nodded. 'Partly; I mistreated her and I was sorry for that. She got her vengeance, though, but all that's in the past now and I want you to forget, as I've done. She's well and truly out of my life now.'

'And you want me in now?'

A hand spurred through his hair in frustration. 'Not the way you make it sound, Verity, as if I'm exchanging one for the other. It isn't like that. I want you in my life and I intend to have you.'

'And ... and when you've finished with me, will you pay me off the same way?'

She didn't know why she was doing this, pushing him, pushing him. Then she knew: if she shoved hard enough he might tell her exactly why he wanted her in his life, because up until now she had only her own feeble hopes to hang on to.

'I'm going to treat that remark with the contempt it deserves,' he told her darkly, 'and ignore it.' His thumbs dug into her shirt. 'Get dressed, Verity. We're going out to dinner to discuss how quickly you can move in with me, because I'm not taking no for an answer.'

She went to the bathroom to shower and dress and wondered at her sudden timidity in standing up to him. She had every reason to refuse his request. She didn't like being manipulated, for one thing; she didn't like his out-and-out insistence that she go and live with him. But three things had swayed her reasoning. Sarah was indeed out of his life now, that was the first; the second was that silly, silly word, darling. He had never said it before and it gave her hope that he might care for her more deeply than he could admit. The third was her own deep love for him. If she lived with him and showed it he might learn to love her ...

'You look beautiful,' he breathed when she came out of the bedroom in amethyst silk. He took her hands and raised them to his lips and kissed them tenderly.

Verity smiled up at him and would have been filled with happiness at the look in his soft grey eyes but she still had so many doubts and insecurities to overcome. She would need to know he truly loved her before telling him about his baby, and that could take time that she didn't have. And if she found he didn't love her she would never be able to tell him, and that was one reason why he wasn't going to get all his own way and reason enough for her to be very firm with him. He said he didn't bargain but he would have to, because she had to think of herself and the baby in the event that the novelty of his having her in his life wore off the way it obviously had with his last lover.

CHAPTER EIGHT

'I WANT to carry on working, Rupert. It's the only way for me.' It was imperative to have something to fall back on if it didn't work out.

Verity leaned back and let the waiter serve her with gingered prawns. It was a lovely restaurant in Holland Park. One of Rupert's favourites, of course, one she couldn't afford to frequent if she scrimped for a month.

She leaned forward when the waiter had left but not before she had seen that tell-tale darkening of Rupert's eyes.

'And don't argue,' she went on, 'because it will be useless. I like my job and want to keep it.'

'What are you trying to prove—your independence, your feminism, or are you just thinking that I'm the sort to take you over, body and soul?'

'Well, you haven't done a bad job so far. You've insisted on taking me out to dinner.'

He smiled. 'Surely not against your will?'

'No, I was starving, as it happens, and quite willing to be manipulated that far, but I want my independence, Rupert, you must understand that.'

'So why agree to live with me?'

'I haven't yet.'

His eyes softened. 'You might not have said the words but you will, won't you?'

'Depends.' She was still playing cat and mouse, more with herself than him. One minute she was

143

convinced it would work, the next she was mortally afraid it wouldn't.

'Terms again?'

'All agreements state terms, Rupert, even marriage. To love, honour and obey and all that.'

He grinned suddenly. 'That sounds like my sort of terms. Marry me, then.'

Verity raised a cynical brow. She didn't take that proposal seriously, as she knew it wasn't meant that way.

'With the emphasis on the obey bit, no doubt?' She shook her head. 'Marriage wouldn't make any difference to what I want, Rupert. I want to keep my job because for one thing I enjoy it, and another is that if this cohabiting doesn't work I don't want to be left high and dry.'

His eyes glinted and she knew he was losing his cool. 'With that attitude it doesn't stand much of a chance from the off.'

'What attitude?'

'Think positive, not negative, Verity. Think it's going to work and it will.'

'Fairyland,' she countered drily. 'Do you know the divorce rate?'

'We're not getting married, are we?'

It was a rhetorical question and she was glad she hadn't taken that silly proposal seriously in the first place.

'Definitely not, and I'm not sure our living together would work.'

'Well, it will have to, because I'm insisting on it,' he told her firmly.

'Such macho treatment,' she sighed theatrically. 'You really scare me. I can see I'm going to have to take a course in subservience.'

There was a weighty pause before he said very seriously, 'Why are you doing this, Verity, why are you being so flippant and cynical about it all?'

Seriousness suddenly hit her too. 'I'm sorry,' she offered quietly. She didn't know why she was being so offhand about it all—defence possibly, that fear of being left high and dry. Rupert wanted her to live with him, wasn't it enough for her?

Panic suddenly clawed at her. She couldn't do it and it was because of this baby. It wasn't fair to him. A life with conditions he'd led with Sarah; well, there would be conditions with her as well when she told him about the baby. Not ones imposed by her, but emotional bonds he'd feel duty-bound to uphold. No, not that way.

'Do I get time to think it over?' she murmured at last.

'Not one second,' he told her firmly. 'I want you in my life, here and now——'

'I can't just up and move in——'

'Why? You don't own your flat; just give in your notice and move out.'

Her eyes narrowed. 'How did you know I don't own my own flat?'

He smiled secretively. 'What a short memory you have. You told me at Stuart's dinner party.'

Verity tilted her head. 'Funny you should remember that and not my name when I first arrived at El Molino. You called me Beryl.'

'It was a slip of the tongue,' he said and she didn't know whether to believe him or not but there was one way of finding out.

'Were you attracted to me the first time you met me at Stuart's and Angie's dinner party?'

He looked at her in surprise. 'You've never asked me that before.'

'No, and I've never asked you if you like your porridge made with sugar or salt but it's one of the things I'll find out if I agree to live with you.'

'And is that question relevant to your decision?'

'Not really. I don't suppose I'll ever cook you porridge—— '

'The first question,' he interrupted tersely.

'Silly me. No, it isn't relevant, but I'd just like to know.'

Rupert leaned across the table and his eyes were suddenly teasing. 'Yes, I was attracted to you, so strongly that I wanted to drag you away from the party and make love to you in the back of my car. Happy?'

Verity held his eyes, searching for the truth and finding it without any trouble. Of course he'd been attracted—sex again. No, she wasn't happy.

'Why didn't you, then?' she asked brazenly.

'Because I knew why we were both there. You were bait and I wasn't biting.'

'Because you were still involved with Sarah?'

His eyes darkened. 'No, I just like to pick my own women and not have them thrust upon me. Now, if this is question-and-answer time, it's my turn. Would you have come with me to the back of my car?'

'No, I damned well wouldn't!'

'Why not?'

'Because . . . because I'm not that sort of girl.'

'But you are.' His voice was low and very pointed as he said that.

Verity shifted uncomfortably in her seat. 'I'm not,' she insisted faintly.

'But you are, Verity. I don't mean it in the way that you'd jump into the back of a car with anybody, but we have a strong sexual attraction and it was there from that first night, and that's why you will never accuse me again of wanting you for sex on tap. Look to yourself before passing judgement on me.'

Oh, that statement was so loaded, and she couldn't respond to it because if she did the only answer would be that love was her excuse for her desire for him. She must really have got to him earlier for him to have made such a cutting remark.

'So why do you want me to come and live with you? Upgrading me from back-seat sex?' she asked.

'I upgraded you long ago, but don't get too smart, Verity, there's more to life than bedding. Apart from the fact that we are good together in bed, I happen to like you around.'

'That's something,' she breathed exaggeratedly, as if it were a weight off her mind. 'But we'll hardly see each other. We'll both be out all day.'

He smiled. 'Not me. I've decided to work from home. The screenplay turned out well and I want to do more.'

'What about your companies?'

'I keep slaves. So are you really determined to carry on your work when you come and live with me?'

So he'd given in. Her terms. She felt no triumph, was only slightly galled by the fact that he'd said when not if.

'Yes, I do want to carry on until . . .'

'Until when?' he urged when she didn't go on.

She wondered what he would say or do if she told him the truth—that she would work as far into her pregnancy as was possible.

'Until I change my mind,' she went on. Or until you fall in love with me, she added to herself, knowing she'd give a limb to have that happen.

'So, it's up to me to change it for you,' he said softly and raised his wine glass to hers, and somehow she knew that that was it, confirmation that they would live together.

Verity loved his riverside house at Kew. It was elegant and comfortable and she lacked for nothing, but happiness eluded her.

Their first few days together had been wonderful, with Rupert trying to please her in every way and she him, but the transition from her cosy flat to this elegant home in Kew wasn't easy to adapt to and it was beginning to show. There were staff hovering, for one thing, and she didn't like that because she wasn't used to it and it made her feel uncomfortable.

'I can't help the way I feel,' she told Rupert one morning as she was dressing for work. 'I'd like to get up one morning and go downstairs for my breakfast and not trip over an assortment of grovelling serfs.'

'Dismiss them and serf yourself, then. Fifteen rooms——'

'OK, OK, bloody point taken!' she retorted.

He used every opportunity to get her to give up her job but she was defiant. And work; it wasn't the same. She couldn't admit it to Rupert, or anyone, for that matter, but she was losing interest in it. She had her love and the thoughts of the baby to fill her mind, and somehow that was suddenly more important than her career, a startling discovery but none the less true.

She hadn't told anyone she had moved in with Rupert, and keeping that secret was proving to be a strain as well. In fact, *everything* was a strain and she sensed that Rupert was feeling it too.

'Darling, you look exhausted. If this goes on I'm going to insist you give up your job,' Rupert declared one evening as they were having a drink before dinner.

Here we go again, she grumbled to herself as she sat by the window, gazing out at the grey river. The weather was struggling through spring and she wasn't seeing much of it. It was usually dusk by the time she got home after work.

'Career, not job,' she corrected stiffly, 'and you insist on far too much, Rupert.'

She held the gin and tonic he had handed her but didn't touch it. She couldn't drink it, the doctor had said not to. He'd also said to ease up; she was stressed, and that wasn't healthy for the baby. She was only two and a half months pregnant and it felt like ten, and the thought of the rest wasn't particularly enthralling.

'I want you to be happy,' he murmured.

Love me, then, she wanted to cry, make it easy for me to have to tell you about our baby. She looked up at him and smiled faintly. 'I'm sorry,' she breathed regrettably. 'I am trying, but...but...'

Greta, the housekeeper, came in to tell them dinner was ready. Resentfully and without another word Verity got to her feet, and Rupert frowned at her as she walked towards the door. He caught her arm.

'What's wrong now?' he asked impatiently.

She snatched her arm away. 'Nothing. I'm just tired, and for God's sake don't tell me to give up work again—you've pushed that one to death and back!'

She walked away from him, knowing in her heart that it was all her fault. The gulf was widening and she wasn't doing anything to stop it.

That night he didn't come to bed till two in the morning and when he did he didn't make love to her. Verity lay awake all night and stared into the darkness and listened to the night sounds.

She had everything and nothing. Rupert was always there for her and yet he wasn't. She felt that these last few days he'd had something on his mind but she hadn't asked what, and that was her failing, not his.

The next morning she didn't go to work. She was tired and felt slightly sick, and worry was beginning to take its toll. Rupert would notice her condition before long and she wasn't ready for that yet.

'I've a few days' leave,' she told him when he queried why she wasn't rushing around at the last minute as she usually was every morning.

It was partly true. She had some leave coming and would phone Alan later and tell him she wanted it now.

'Good. I'll take a break with you——'

'No!' Verity sat up in bed, her heart hammering. She had a doctor's appointment later. 'No, it isn't necessary, and didn't you say you had a lot of work on this week?'

'It can wait. Why don't we go out for the day?'

Verity smiled. 'No, it would put you behind, Rupert. I've masses to do and...and I'll keep popping into the study to see you.'

He seemed placated but she noticed the slight frown on his brow and later she thought she knew why.

It was that phone call. Verity was down in the sitting-room overlooking the river and reading the morning's papers, and the phone was ringing incessantly. Normally she didn't answer the phone because it was never for her and usually there was someone else to pick it up anyway. She remembered that Greta was out shopping. She reached out and picked up the receiver just as Rupert picked up the extension in his study. She was about to put it down when she heard Rupert's voice.

'Sarah, we've been through all this before. You're wasting your time... I'm sorry...'

Slowly, silently and desperately Verity put down the receiver. There was a cold sweat on her brow and her legs would hardly carry her weight as she rushed to the cloakroom.

She was sick and then sick again, and then she leaned her hot forehead against the mirror over the sink. She had known...all along she had known that Sarah was still with Rupert, in his mind and his heart. They were still in touch with each other and perhaps they were still seeing each other and... and... Her anguish took her tormented thoughts further. Rupert had suggested they go out for the day because he knew Sarah would ring him and there was a chance she would find out... Verity didn't know what to do. To tackle him or... or what?

'Verity!'

She jerked herself away from the mirror and stared at her reflection. She couldn't tackle it yet; no, not yet. Oh, God, she looked awful and felt it; she was pale and colourless.

'Verity, I have to go out,' he told her briskly as she met him on the curving stairway, she going up and he coming down. There was no eye contact, just Rupert rushing past her, pulling his leather jacket on.

He was going to see her, that woman. She just had to pick up the phone and he went running!

'What time will you be back?' She hadn't intended to sound so demanding but it came out that way.

'When I'm ready,' he told her shortly and went out of the front door.

Half an hour later Verity went out herself after calling a mini-cab. She just had to get out of that house, *his* house with Sarah's lingering perfume. She hated him for this, demanding that she live with him and then carrying on with his ex-lover, except she might not be his ex-lover; they might never have stopped seeing each other!

'Verity!' Rupert called out as soon as she returned, five hours later and so tired that she was fit to drop.

He came out into the hall. 'Where have you been? I've been worried...Verity, what the devil have you done?'

Her hand went instinctively up to her new shorter-length hair. She'd had it cut and restyled and she'd had a facial and a manicure, because that was what kept mistresses did. She looked at Rupert and burst into tears.

'Darling...'

'Don't darling me!' she sobbed, and dived for the stairs. She'd had a horribly stressful day, spending his money, trying to make herself into something she wasn't, and then that painful blood test at the doctor's and another warning to ease up. She had gone back to her flat—contrary to what Rupert had believed, she had kept it on—and it was cold and empty without her personal things there. She had felt homesick on top of everything else and so so lonely.

'Darling, what's wrong?' Rupert asked, sitting on the edge of the huge double bed she had thrown herself on.

He eased her up into his arms and held her tightly. 'Did you think I'd be mad at you for having your lovely hair cut off? I'm not, treasure, I adore it.'

'I hate it!' she sobbed. Her hand came up and rubbed at the new eyeshadow that widened and deepened and added allure to her eyes—so the assistant had told her. 'I...I wish I hadn't had it done.'

'It's lovely, makes you look sixteen and in-credibly desirable.' His hand slid into the bouncy curves and it so painfully reminded her of the time he had first touched her hair at El Molino. She wished they were back there, where life had no outside interferences. Just the two of them, co-cooned so intimately together.

'Verity,' he breathed huskily and moved her face so he could kiss her lips. And she let him because the day had been so awful and she wanted his comfort and his lovemaking. He kissed away her tears and slowly started to undress her. All the grim questions she wanted grim answers for lay buried under the avalanche of the sensations he was rushing her with. His hands were so warm and tan-talising on her rounded breasts, and his lips blazed a trail of white heat as they ran over her stomach. His breathing quickened and was roughened by his rising desire and it all gathered up to swamp all else from her heart and mind.

She didn't know why she thought this time was different from the other times they had made love. She imagined that Rupert was more tender and that his kisses were more ardent and he was more gentle with her when he entered her. He was a beautiful lover, always surprising her with a touch, a caress, and this time was no different in that way. She thought he had discovered every secret part of her, but there was always one more delight.

She was crying as she reached her climax, silent tears that he would never see. He didn't come with her but stilled himself as her muscles spasmed around him, enhancing her pleasure and then moving slowly inside her once again, his breathing now more ragged and drugged with sensation. When he came she clasped him to her, raking her hands in his hair, urging her hips into his, silently saying the words she so longed to speak, that she loved him and always would and would give years of her life to hear him speak the same to her.

Later they went down to dinner, and Verity watched him across the table. She was searching again, for some sign of what made him tick. She wondered if he had made love to Sarah today and bit her lip at the sordidness of such a thought.

'Where did you go today?' she asked after Greta had dished up delicious marinated lamb and rice.

He looked up from his food and she thought she saw guilt in his eyes; no, she was *certain* she'd seen guilt.

'You going out to work every day certainly has its advantages,' he told her teasingly. 'If you were home all day you could be one of those possessive wives questioning every move I make.'

'But I'm not your wife. Was that another of your slips of the tongue or a Freudian slip?' Dear God, but she was sailing close to the wind.

'It could have been a disguised proposal,' he suggested pointedly.

Her stomach tightened. 'Was it?' she murmured, hope rising and falling and swishing around inside her till she felt sick and disorientated

'Do you want it to be?' he asked, those eyes of his offering no such promise.

Her heart spasmed defensively. What game were they playing here? Russian roulette? Someone was going to get the bullet and it wasn't going to be her.

'I've told you before, I don't care a fig for marriage.' She carried on eating, not wanting to look into those eyes and read relief.

'I have to go away for a couple of days,' he said at last, and Verity felt the awful day crowd in on her with more awfulness. First the phone call and then his rushing out, and her despair over Sarah, resulting in that childish display of attention-seeking with her hair and face and nails and then . . . then his beautiful, poignant lovemaking, making up in advance for this bombshell, no doubt.

'Where?' she asked, as if she didn't really care, except she did and life was getting worse by the minute.

'New York. I'd take you with me, but I'm only staying overnight and you'd be bored with the meetings I have to attend.'

Don't even give me the option to refuse, she dismally thought.

She didn't even get the chance to pack for him—Greta did that. She didn't even get the chance to drive him to the airport—he had a chauffeur for that. So what was her damned role in his life—to buffet his ego, to warm his bed?

She was desolate when he left the next morning after kissing her goodbye. She tried to make conversation with Greta in the kitchen but Greta was Austrian and, though her English was good, they were continents apart in conversation. But she learned how to make apple strudel, Vienna-style, so at least that was something.

The phone rang at midday and Verity rushed to it before Greta. Concorde was supersonic, but surely not even with a tail-wind behind it . . .

'Hello; hello.' There was silence the other end and Verity's heart iced, and when the receiver clicked down she instinctively knew that the caller had been Sarah. Then realisation surged through her: well, at least she wasn't on her way to New York with Rupert. She forced herself to feel happy at that thought but when the next call came five minutes later her heart chilled frighteningly.

'Look, who is this? Just say what you want...'

There was faint breathing from the other end and Verity's fist tightened around the receiver.

'He's not here,' she cried. 'Rupert isn't here. He's away...'

The line went dead and Verity was trembling as she put the receiver down. That had been a dumb thing to say. The caller could have been a burglar checking to see if anyone was at home. For once she was glad there were staff around.

Later Greta announced that she was going out for a couple of hours and had left her a cold lunch in the fridge. The two cleaners had already left, and suddenly Verity was alone in the house, alone and very nervous. There were more unproductive calls till Verity was nearly tearing her hair out with anguish by the time Greta returned. She said nothing about the calls, though, after deciding that she was over-reacting, but nevertheless her stomach somersaulted when the next one came.

'Mr Scott on the phone for you,' Greta told her later, popping her head round the door. 'I'll make you some tea and the strudel, yes?'

Verity thanked him and dived to the phone, her pulses racing with relief.

'Rupert!' she wailed.

'What's wrong, darling?'

She'd planned on being angry with him; had even rehearsed her words and her accusations, but it all drained from her lips as she heard his voice.

'Nothing,' she breathed softly, clutching at her chest. 'I'm just relieved you got there safely.'

He laughed and then he said words she had so longed to hear.

'Verity, I'm missing you like crazy. I wish I'd brought you with me.' His voice was low and very slightly unsteady.

'I wish too,' she murmured.

'Are you happy, darling?'

Verity nodded and bit her lip. 'Yes, just a bit worried about you arriving.'

Where were the accusations and the demands for the truth? But what truth? Perhaps there wasn't any, perhaps she was being silly, her nerves so taut and stressed that she was willing to believe anything—that he was still seeing Sarah.

'I meant long-term happy, Verity. You've seemed so preoccupied these last few days. I only want your happiness, you know.'

'Oh, Rupert,' she breathed. Suddenly her eyes filled with tears and she wanted to tell him about the phone calls and her fears, but it was painful, too painful, and the words just wouldn't come.

'Verity...' He went silent and she could almost hear his inward struggle, as if he wanted to say so much, but it just wouldn't come out. She helped him.

'I'm missing you too, Rupert,' she breathed huskily. 'Listen, I've... I've decided I don't want to work any more.' Her statement was as much a surprise to herself as it was to Rupert.

His laughter was soft and relieved. 'I'm glad to hear that and I look forward to hearing a lot more from you when I get back.'

'Oh, Rupert, I wish you were here. There's so much I need to know and so much I want to say.'

'It won't be long, darling,' he soothed. 'I'll be back with you tomorrow.'

They were an ocean apart, but somehow that gulf between them was narrowing. Verity didn't know why. After those phone calls she should be desperate, but hearing his voice like this, soft and warm and tender, as if that flight across the Atlantic had made him realise what he had, filled her with hope.

'Hurry back,' she urged. 'The house is bleak without you.'

'You have the staff for company,' he laughed.

She made a snorting sound and he laughed again, and then his voice turned mysterious. 'After you've put the phone down, go to my desk, and in the top drawer you'll find something I bought for you a couple of days ago. I wasn't going to give it to you till I got back, but you sound as if you need a bit of an upper.'

'A present?' she breathed.

'More like a promise,' he told her quietly, and then added, 'I have to go, Verity; I'll call you later.'

'I'll wait up,' she said quickly.

'I'd rather you took the call in bed and then I can imagine . . . well, you know.'

'Yes, I know,' she grinned.

She hugged herself as she went to the study after putting the phone down. Something had happened in the relationship, something too subtle for analysis at the moment. It was odd, but after hearing his voice so very far away she felt reassured rather than anything. Those calls she'd presumed had come from Sarah could have been wrong numbers or someone messing around, a troubled person who got a thrill from worrying the life out of people.

'Oh, Rupert,' she breathed, staring down into the black suede box with its black silk lining. Carefully she lifted out the platinum chain with its solitaire diamond pendant and held it up to the light.

It was beautiful, simple and yet quite exquisite. Shakily Verity pressed it to her lips. Diamonds were forever. He'd said a promise...

'I'm sorry, Miss Verity...'

Verity swung to the door, shocked at the sudden commotion and Greta's apologetic outburst. The pendant slid from her fingers and plopped to the floor.

'So, you're the new bed warmer,' came a silky drawl from behind Greta.

Verity knew right away who she was. Tall, elegant, stunningly beautiful with jet hair that moved as she walked. She came straight up to Verity and would have done an inspection circuit if it weren't for Rupert's leather chair blocking her way.

'It's all right, Greta,' Verity assured the nervous housekeeper. Verity clenched her fists at her side as Greta gave her an apologetic look and backed out of the room.

'What do you want?' Verity bravely asked.

'Do you know who I am?' The woman asked with a cynical smile on her lovely face.

'Yes, you're Sarah,' Verity said.

The beautiful Sarah gave a knowing smile. 'So he talks about me to you, does he?'

'Not really,' Verity told her coolly. 'But when you live with someone you find out about their past.' She laid emphasis on the past and Sarah was on to it straight away.

'I'll never be his past, dear——'

'Don't call me dear,' Verity cut in sharply. 'The name is Verity.'

There was a long pause as Sarah eyed her up and down again. 'Well, Verity,' she drawled at last, 'you and your presence here surprise me. Rupert doesn't go for blondes, and frankly I didn't think he'd enter into another affair so quickly after me.'

Verity held her temper because to let rip at this woman would be playing into her hands.

'What did you come here for?' she asked, feigning uninterest.

'I came to see Rupert, but it's obvious he isn't here.'

'You knew that. I told you when you phoned.' She watched her reaction to that and in an instant knew by the darkening of her eyes that the calls had come from her, and now she was here because curiosity had spurred her.

Sarah didn't like being caught out and her eyes narrowed angrily. 'Well, much as it galls me to have to ask, when will he be back?'

'Tomorrow, but perhaps I can help you in the meantime.' Verity's fingernails were almost imbedded in her palms. She wished she would go because she was afraid she wouldn't be able to contain herself much longer.

'You could help yourself by getting out from where you don't belong.'

Verity forced a confident smile, though she didn't feel it. 'What I do is nothing to do with you, and what Rupert does is no longer a concern of yours, Sarah.'

'You have half a point. You are none of my business because you won't be around for long, but Rupert will always be of concern to me, as I am to him. I'm a part of his life and no one can change that.'

'I think he already has. He's told me you're nothing——'

'Then he's a liar!' Sarah suddenly stormed. 'And you're a fool to think you can take my place. Rupert and I have ties that can never be broken. Oh, he's tried, but I'm not having any of that——'

'What do you want, more money?' Verity's eyes blazed now. She wasn't going to take all this garbage from this woman.

'Money!' Sarah laughed spitefully. 'No money in the world will compensate for what that bastard's done to me and our child...'

Verity's stomach tipped and she gripped the edge of the desk to steady herself.

'Child?' she croaked.

Sarah suddenly looked so triumphant that she seemed to swell with it.

'I can see that's shocked you. A small part of his life he failed to tell you about?' she simpered cruelly.

Verity just stared blindly at her. 'He ... he didn't say,' she whispered.

'We have a baby daughter, a daughter he doesn't want to know about, never did want to know about. He told me to get out when I was five months pregnant, when it was too late for an abortion. He didn't want to know about fatherhood or even being a husband; all he lives for is his damned business empire...'

Verity swayed and righted herself and closed herself off from the outside world. She was only vaguely aware of the rest of what Sarah was screaming at her. She remembered her own cold indifference as she asked Sarah to leave, and she remembered thinking as Sarah stormed out of the house that she felt desperately sorry for the poor woman; the rest was a red mist of anguish. Sarah loved Rupert and was desperate to get him back. She had a child to cope with, Rupert's child, and he hadn't wanted to know, and that mist thickened and engulfed her.

Slowly Verity went upstairs to the bedroom she shared with Rupert and shakily pulled her clothes from the wardrobe.

Funny, but she was glad Sarah had come, because now she knew that Rupert would never marry her or love her or care two hoots for the child she was carrying. And deep down hadn't she known this all along? Some sixth sense must have warned her to keep her flat on, and her job. Thank God. For once in her life uncertainty had paid off.

CHAPTER NINE

'WHAT'S wrong?' Alan asked as Verity shakily put down the telephone receiver. 'Bad news?'

Dazedly Verity looked up at him hovering over her desk. 'No... no, just something a bit unexpected has cropped up. Personal, I'm afraid, so don't waste your breath asking me what.'

She pushed her trembling fingers through her hair and stood up. 'I'm sorry, Alan, I've got to ask for this afternoon off as well.' If he objected she was going to have to give in her notice, because if her worst fears were realised there would be a lot more of these missed working hours.

'No problem. I didn't expect you in this morning anyway. I thought you said you wanted a few days of your leave; you only had two.'

'I was bored.' Verity told him, crossing to the window and desperately wanting to be alone to get her thoughts together. She'd slept badly, as the flat had taken ages to heat up, and there was only one place to go when she had got up and that was work. She wanted to carry on as before, and calling the doctor for the results of her blood test was part of her normality plan. The doctor wanted to see her today. She had a rare blood group and, though there was no cause for alarm, they wanted to keep a close eye on her throughout her pregnancy... and there would be tests on the unborn baby.

'Are you sure there's nothing wrong? You haven't been right for ages,' Alan persisted.

Verity moved back to her desk. 'Just tired.'

'Can you untire yourself for tonight? Stuart and Angie are having a dinner party. Stuart's phoned you at home every night, but you're never there.' He grinned knowingly as he added, 'Perhaps that's why you're looking so washed out. Who's the new man in your life, or is it men?'

'Shut up, Alan,' Verity ordered scathingly. 'You can ring Stuart for me and tell him what to do with his dinner parties.' She suddenly smiled over-sweetly. 'No, don't bother; why should you have all the fun? I'll tell him myself.'

'You're not still holding a grudge over that Scott business, are you?' he laughed.

Verity paralysed him with a fast-freeze look. 'How is my cousin, by the way?' she asked, lifting a file from her desk and flicking it open. She really didn't want to know, having troubles enough of her own, but he was still her cousin.

'He's fine. Business picking up and it looks as if he might get Scott's advertising after all——'

Verity tensed and lifted her head to look at Alan. 'What the hell do you mean?' she blurted sharply.

Alan frowned at her sudden outburst but didn't remark on it. 'Scott's put a new man in as his advertising director, and Stuart's approached him and it's looking good.'

Verity desensitised herself. For a moment she thought Rupert might have given Stuart the advertising because of her, but highly unlikely from a man who was insensitive enough not to want his own child.

She didn't go back to work after the doctor's appointment. She was too tired and stunned. She'd never known about her rare blood group, but that wasn't surprising. She'd never had an accident or a serious illness that warranted a blood test. It wasn't serious but could be for the baby if the father's blood wasn't compatible. Somehow she had fluffed her way out of that question—what was the father's blood group? She'd said she'd find out, but how? Short of cutting his throat and taking her own sample . . .

She sighed heavily as she drove home, taking it easy in the rush-hour traffic, as the warning the doctor had issued her with had rather worried her. She was verging on anaemia and had a pile of vitamins to take, and she'd been told to ease up. Some chance of that, she thought ruefully as she parked in the square outside the flat. She was going to be a single parent and would have to support this child.

As she stepped into her hallway the phone started ringing. It was Alan.

'Verity, Rupert Scott has been in the office and practically blew a gasket when I told him you weren't here but at home.'

Oh, God. Verity flopped down on a chair and held her head in her free hand. She should have left a note, something to prepare him for this. But why? He didn't deserve any consideration for anything!

'What did he want?' she uttered weakly, considering that it was a rather stupid question.

'I might ask you the same thing. He didn't say, but he was livid. What the hell is going on? Did you walk out of El Molino with his Snoopy toothbrush?'

Oh, more than that!

'I have to go, Alan. I'll tell you all about it to-morrow.' She put the phone down and her hand was shaking as she did it. And she probably would tell him all about it. She had no one else to turn to and over the next few months she would need his support.

Rupert would come here, she knew that for certain. You couldn't just walk out on Rupert Scott. She was prepared, or thought she was, when she heard him leaning on the doorbell.

She opened the door and in that second lost her nerve completely, and all she had practised in her head went out of it like a puff of wind.

He stepped into the hallway, half-bull, half-man, grasped her arm and pushed her into the small sitting-room. When they got there he swivelled her to face him. His eyes were black and thunderous and his facial muscles were contorted with fury.

'This is a kick where it hurts, Verity Brooks!' His hand waved around the room. 'Why, Verity, why keep this place on? You had no damned intention of making a life with me, did you? Oh, no, milk me for what I could offer and——'

'Rupert!' Verity cried so harshly that he stopped mid-sentence. 'Stop this, it's doing no good——'

'It's a bloody release,' Rupert blazed, 'because I could kill you for this!'

'Go ahead!' she cried. 'Worse things could happen!'

His eyes locked with hers in a painful look that tore at Verity's heart. There was sorrow there in his

eyes with the fury but she wasn't going to be fooled
by that. She thought of Sarah, and an image of her
and their child rose so vividly within her that she
wasn't afraid any more.

'Why?' Rupert pleaded, his voice hoarse. 'Why
are you here and not waiting at home for me?'

'What home?' she questioned defensively, her
eyes wide and clear. 'Your home maybe, but certainly not mine. *This* is my home.'

'My home is yours; I never thought of offering
you anything less, but when you agreed to come
and live with me I didn't dream for a minute you'd
be so chillingly deceptive. How could you have kept
this place on, and why?'

Now she was the guilty party. Where was the
justice in this world?

'I kept it on because...' She faltered. She had
been wrong to do it. She should have loved and
trusted him more and had faith enough that it
would work out, but she hadn't, and on reflection
it was one of her better decisions; otherwise, where
could she have gone after Sarah's revelations?

'Because what? You were so unsure of my feelings
for you?' he questioned dully.

She forced the answer through her burning lips.
'Yes, Rupert,' she whispered truthfully. 'I was so
unsure of your feelings. You've never given me
reason to think there were any.'

He stepped back from her as if she had shot him.
He turned away and stood by the window and stared
out at the small green opposite, raking his fingers
through his hair.

'You didn't look hard enough, Verity.' He sighed
raggedly. 'And you couldn't have had any in-

tention of looking because you kept this place on.
So why are you here now, why now, of all times?'
he asked quietly, his anger seeming to have
evaporated.

'Because . . . because it didn't work out.'

'I thought it was working out,' he grated, half
turning towards her. 'I understood your insecurities at first. Didn't I do enough to make you feel
happy and secure?'

She nodded bleakly. 'Yes, but . . . but it wasn't
enough.'

'Living a life of luxury isn't enough? You had
everything with me. I could give you everything.'

Love was all I wanted, Verity whispered inwardly.

He suddenly reached into his pocket and drew
out the diamond pendant and held it up. 'Wasn't
this enough?'

The pain was indescribable as she stared at the
beautiful jewel. Rupert Scott bought people and
paid them off when he'd finished with them, just
as he had done with Sarah.

Her eyes were iceberg-cold as she glared at him.
'I'm not to be bought, Rupert.'

'Bought!' he raged. 'What the hell did you think
I was buying, your bloody body?'

She shook her head miserably. She felt so weak
and insignificant against his anger. And the pain
in her heart prevented her from spilling out what
she should. That he was a liar and a bastard for
what he'd done to Sarah, and what hope had she
with him when she was in the same position as his
unfortunate ex-mistress had been? Carrying his
child, a child he wouldn't want?

When she didn't fight back he suddenly came to her, gently took her upper arms and pressed his thumbs into her sensitive flesh. 'Is that why you took flight, because you thought the gift was...was some sort of payment for your services?'

'Oh, God, no!' she breathed hotly, her eyes filling with tears. 'I didn't think that, not that ... and you shouldn't have suggested it, Rupert, you shouldn't have.'

His grip tightened. 'What am I to think, then? I get home and find your clothes gone, none of the staff knowing where you are, the pendant discarded on the floor of the study. I drove to your office, only to learn you are here. What the hell have I done to deserve this?'

Verity hung her head. Why did he make her feel so guilty when he was the one who was wicked and evil?

'I...I had to come here. I didn't...I didn't want to be with you any more.' She looked up at him then and it was the bravest thing she had ever done. She held his eyes. 'It wasn't working, Rupert——'

He shook her. 'It was, you know damned well it was. When I phoned you from New York it was good. I felt that something had changed and when I got back you would care as much for me as I care for you.'

The tears spilled from Verity's eyes then and Rupert smeared them away with the backs of his fingers.

'You do care, don't you, Verity? I know it. I feel it, but something has happened; tell me what?'

At last he had made an admittance of his deep feeling for her but it was too late, and she couldn't tell him why because it had all happened in his life before and no good had come out of it. She could imagine this very scenario happening between him and Sarah, and Sarah's saying that there was a baby and his going cold and thrusting her away. . .

Verity tore herself from his grasp and stood in front of the fireplace, staring down at the unlit fire. She felt as cold and dismal as the dormant coals.

'I'm . . . I'm sorry I left in such a hurry, without a proper explanation,' she murmured. 'But put it down to cowardice. I didn't want to face you.' She stared bleakly at the mantelpiece and couldn't face him now. 'I want it to end, this affair. I don't want to live with you any more. I want my own life, not yours. I'm sorry if I hurt you by keeping this flat on, but I suppose I must have known all the time that it wouldn't work.' She swallowed hard and wondered how she had ever got that out without completely breaking down.

She flinched as he came up behind her and touched her neck. 'I don't want it to finish this way, darling. I want you to come back with me now and we'll talk it over——'

'There's nothing to talk over,' she husked, wishing he wouldn't stroke the back of her neck like that. 'I won't change my mind. I want to stay here and live my life, not yours.'

Dear God, she prayed he wouldn't feel the tremor of despair that threaded through her and the tremor of reluctant desire that rose as he caressed her neck. She couldn't hate him. She could hate what he did, but he was still the man she loved and the father of the child within her.

She felt something cold around her neck, and her hand came up and she felt the beautiful single diamond in the hollow of her throat. Rupert was fastening the clasp at the back of her neck. Verity's fingers closed over the pendant and she closed her eyes in pain. The necklace seemed to sear her flesh. She wanted to tear it away but couldn't. Her whole body seemed to be paralysed in agony.

Slowly Rupert turned her to him. 'Wear this, Verity. I want you to have it, and please don't think of it as some sort of payment. I bought it because I love you...'

Verity's heart stopped and her legs melted. Oh, God, why was life so cruel and why was he? He loved her and she loved him, but he had done something so unforgivable to Sarah and he'd do the same to her if she allowed it.

He lowered his mouth to hers and kissed her lips so tenderly that she nearly allowed herself to clasp him to her and tell him all she had always wanted to say to him. That she loved him and only wanted him in her life. The kiss intensified and his body was pressed so hard to hers that she felt every beat of his heart twinned with hers. This was all she had ever wanted, his admission of love, but it was impossible now, impossible because of what Sarah had told her. He might love her but he wouldn't love another child forced upon him. He didn't want the one he had.

'A promise,' he murmured, 'it was a promise, Verity. To love, honour and obey——'

'Oh, no!' She tore herself away then and faced him bitterly. 'Don't say things like that!' she cried painfully. 'Don't say things you don't mean.'

He grasped her again, tightly. 'I do mean it!' he grated. 'I love you and I want to marry you——'

'You'd make any sort of promise to save your face, wouldn't you?' she flamed, her anger spurred by the pain within her breast. 'You say you love me but it's just a sham and nothing more. You just can't bear the thought that I chose to walk out on you. You didn't throw me out the way you threw Sarah out, and that's really got to your insufferable pride, hasn't it?'

'I have no damned pride where you're concerned,' he grated through his clenched teeth, 'but my God I had some where she was concerned. That's why she's out and you were in——'

'Like trading in a car for a more up-to-date model!' Verity cried back. 'You haven't any feelings, Rupert. If you had you would have been more compassionate to Sarah, you would...' Her voice trailed away and the silence that stepped into its place was heavy and ponderous.

Seconds later Rupert spoke heavily. 'I didn't come here to discuss Sarah, and you had no right to bring something up that is no concern of yours. I came here to take you back home with me——'

'No!' Verity cried.

It was the most final no in the world, and Rupert recognised it as such.

'Is that your last word?' he breathed heavily.

She nodded, because she couldn't speak.

His expressionless grey eyes lingered for only another fleeting second, and then he turned on his heel and walked out.

* * *

Verity stretched out her hand and turned the alarm clock to face her. Only midnight; she'd thought it was much later. She lay back on her pillows. This was how life was going to be in future—one long drag.

She sat up suddenly as the doorbell went, persistently. She'd know that ring anywhere.

'I've nothing more to say to you,' she called through the door. 'Go away and leave me alone.'

'Don't make me angry, Verity; open this door before I kick it in.'

She did because she had neighbours. Rupert brushed past her and went straight to the bedroom.

'Where is it?'

'What? *My* new trade-in?'

She leaned in the doorway, surprisingly calm as she watched him, surprisingly uncalm, searching her wardrobe.

'Your sense of humour is sick. I'm the only man in your life and you'd better believe it.'

Verity's stomach tightened. 'That's what you think.'

'It's what I know.' He hauled an overnight bag from the wardrobe and tossed it on the bed. 'Take what you need for your immediate needs and I'll send someone over for the rest of your stuff tomorrow.'

'Is this a kidnap?' she drawled sarcastically.

'No, this is reclamation of what is rightly mine— you!'

'I belong to myself——'

'Quit it, Verity,' he snapped, 'and don't give me all that "I'm my own person" rubbish. You're coming back with me because it's where you belong.' He wrenched open a drawer of her dressing-table and started pulling out her underwear.

Verity lurched across the room and her hand tightened over his.

'How dare you dominate me this way, bursting in here and being so bloody bolshie? Leave my knickers alone!'

'Would that I could!' His eyes softened and glinted with humour, and if her heart weren't tearing so badly she would have laughed with him.

'Why are you doing this?' she blurted, pulling her hand away from his.

'Because now I know what's driving you so crazy.'

Her pulses accelerated. He couldn't know. Nobody knew.

'What?' she uttered huskily.

'Sarah. When I came here earlier I didn't know she had paid you a visit. When I got back to Kew Greta told me she'd called.'

'So?'

'So now I understand.'

'You understand nothing, Rupert!'

'I understand jealousy when I'm faced with it.'

'Jealousy?' Verity screeched.

'Yes, jealousy, and don't try to deny it. You left because——'

'Because she's still a very important part of your life——'

'A part of my past, and not so very important,' he corrected, resuming what he was doing, stuffing her underwear into the hold-all.

'Past, present, future!' Verity stormed. 'And always will be. She still rings you up——'

He straightened himself up and glared at her. 'What are you talking about?'

'Oh, don't deny it. I overheard you talking to her one day and . . . and then you rushed out to meet her and no doubt you made love to her and——'

He gripped her arms. 'Dear God, but I wish I had half as much fun in real life as I have in your imagination!'

'My imagination? I haven't any. It's all fact! I picked up the phone at the same time you did and heard her voice, so don't you even think about denying it.'

'I'm not,' he grated harshly. 'A day doesn't pass when she doesn't call me, making more demands.'

'And you meet them, don't you? You couldn't wait to rush out to her. You tore down the stairs and went tearing out to meet her.'

He looked bemused for a second, as if dredging his memory, and then his face cleared. 'I dashed out to the jewellers to pick up the pendant I was having made for you. I'd called them after speaking with Sarah and it was ready, and I couldn't wait to collect it.'

Paling with shock, Verity gazed up at him and knew by the openness of his eyes that he was telling the truth. But she wasn't elated; somehow to her tortured senses it was worse than ever. Poor Sarah, calling him in another desperate attempt to win back his love for her and her child, and him preoccupied with a gift for the next lady in line.

Verity couldn't bear it and turned away.

'Where are you going?'

She didn't know, just as far from him as was possible. But, while she was clad only in a satin nightie and robe, out into the night wasn't a proposition. She flew to the kitchen and shakily poured a glass of water. She turned when he followed her into the small room.

'Believe me, Verity, I know what you're going through——'

'You don't!' she cried. 'You couldn't possibly know.'

'But I do,' he insisted. 'I understand it all, why you kept this flat on, why you felt so insecure with me. My relationship with Sarah was hanging over you like the sword of Damocles, ever a threat to our love.'

'*Our* love?' she spat. 'Aren't you taking a bit too much for granted? As always!'

He smiled, and that shocked her. 'Are you going to deny you love me? Because forget it if you are. You can only be jealous if you care, Verity, and you care, and that's why you ran away from me. You thought I was still involved with Sarah.'

'And you are and always will be.'

'Only in your mind, certainly not mine.'

How could he be so cruelly dismissive? She shook her head in dismay.

'You bastard,' she breathed raggedly. 'You're the biggest bastard I've ever met.'

He looked shocked at her statement and she was glad. He'd come here tonight to force her back into his home with promises of love and marriage that he couldn't hope to tempt her with because she knew him, knew exactly how hard and cruel he was.

'You'd better go,' she said quietly. 'Because if you don't I might be sorely tempted to kill you.'

He stepped towards her and her body stiffened in defence. He stopped in front of her and lifted her chin.

'Kiss or kill; I wonder which you mean.'

A reminder like that cut painfully into her heart. She tried to step back out of his way but her back was already hard up against the work-surface.

'Don't . . . don't touch me.' It was then that she wanted to cry, for all the past and the dreadful future that lay ahead of her. To love a man like this was a punishment for her sins surely?

He lowered his mouth and his lips skimmed hers, lightly, lovingly and far too late.

She moved her head aside as he threatened to kiss her properly. It angered him and he gripped her by the shoulders.

'What games now, Verity? I love you and want to marry you; what else do you want from me?'

It was all she had ever wanted, but it was all out of sync and too much had happened for her to trust him.

'I . . . can't trust you.' Her eyes filled with tears. 'And I can't give my love . . . my love to a man who . . .' She couldn't finish. The tears choked her nose and her throat.

'A man who what?' he pressed urgently, his eyes searching hers and not understanding.

Somehow she found the strength to tear herself away from him. She couldn't face him and tell him the truth, that she hated him for denying his own daughter and the mother who had borne her.

He caught her at the bedroom door and swung her round so viciously that she feared for her life and that of the baby within her. That fear manifested itself with an angry explosion.

'I hate you, Rupert Scott. You are a cruel, wicked man. You have a daughter...'

She thought he was going to kill her. His eyes hardened to shards of cold metal and his grip was so fierce that her blood stopped coursing.

'A daughter!' he growled, and then his whole body slackened. His face was suddenly grey and then he did something so totally unexpected that it threw her completely.

He gathered her into his arms and held her head against his shoulder. His breathing was heavy and his heart beat loud, and a deep tremor seemed to reverberate through his whole body.

'Dear God, am I going to pay for this for the rest of my life?' he whispered against her.

A great sickness rose inside Verity, so fiercely that she felt dizzy and weak with it. Even now he couldn't face his responsibility; even now he felt he was the wronged one.

She was crushed against him and unable to move, and when he spoke again the dizziness sped upwards and outwards.

'She told you, didn't she?' he whispered. 'But I bet she didn't tell you the child isn't mine——'

Verity came round. Slowly and swimmingly. She was flat out on her bed and someone was sitting on the edge of the bed, bathing her hot brow. The sickness was fading and life was seeping back into her bones.

'Rupert,' she whispered, and blinked open her exhausted eyes. She wished she felt stronger.

'I'm here, darling. I think you fainted, but I've never seen anyone faint before.'

'I fainted,' she murmured. Hadn't the doctor warned her to ease up? She licked her dry lips. 'Tell me it's true, Rupert.'

He smiled down at her. 'It's true, darling; you just went white and slid down and I caught you.'

She tried to laugh but it gurgled in her throat. She felt as if she'd swallowed a hammer.

'I didn't mean that. You said...just before I went silly and feminine...you said the...the child wasn't...' Perhaps she hadn't heard it at all; perhaps wishful thinking had spurred those words to her ears.

Rupert took both her hands and clasped them in his. 'The child isn't mine, darling. Did she tell you it was?'

Verity nodded. 'I couldn't bear it, Rupert, the thought that you didn't want to know your own daughter.' She bit her lip because she had shown no trust in him. 'I...hated you for it. I believed her, you see, and now I hate myself.' The tears welled again and she gulped. 'Oh, Rupert, I believed her, a woman I'd never met before, a woman so screwed up with revenge...'

'Stop it, darling,' he ordered softly. 'Don't torture yourself.'

'But Rupert, why didn't you tell me?' She searched his handsome, drawn face for an answer but didn't find it. He spoke it instead.

'I couldn't talk about it, Verity; maybe in time I would have told you, but the trauma was so deep-seated and she was still putting on such pressure. I've had two years of hell with her and at times I thought it would never be over.'

'You thought it was over when you asked me to come and live with you, though.'

He nodded his dark head. 'After El Molino I knew I wanted you in my life forever, but I wanted the past debris of my life cleared out of the way to be able to offer you all that I wanted to. Even when I knew I was in love with you there, I wasn't emotionally free to offer you anything. When Sarah left——'

'She said you threw her out.'

He gave her a thin smile. 'How could she say anything else? A woman scorned and all that. When she left I supported her, and when the child was born I supported her too, but I wasn't prepared to do that indefinitely. She claimed the child was mine but I knew it wasn't. The relationship had soured long before and I was away at the time she must have conceived.' He shrugged. 'In spite of every-thing, I felt sorry for her, and for a long time I blamed myself. If I'd given her more of my time and love she wouldn't have sought solace else-where, but the feeling wasn't there, you see.'

'I understand,' Verity murmured. 'You felt responsible.'

'And paid for my weakness.'

'It wasn't weakness, Rupert. You must have cared for her at one time and you just couldn't cut off that caring because she had done wrong. And there was a child to be considered, even if it wasn't yours, you wouldn't have seen it suffer.'

'No, it was an innocent being in all this.'

'But when you asked me to live with you you said you were freer.'

'I thought I was. I told Sarah I wasn't prepared to keep her forever and the father should take some responsibility. She then told me who who it was—my advertising director. I sacked him—— '

'Oh.' It hurt her to think he'd done that.

Rupert smiled. 'Don't take that the wrong way, but the bastard was encouraging her to squeeze more money out of me.'

'They were conspiring together?'

He nodded. 'Not a very pleasant discovery,' he husked, and she suddenly realised all that he must have been through. No wonder he had seemed distanced from her at times. And she had actually felt sorry for poor Sarah.

She smiled suddenly at a new realisation.

'What are you smiling at?' Rupert asked, smoothing her hands, which were still clasped in his.

'Well, you've put in a new advertising director and he's having talks with my cousin, Stuart.'

Rupert threw his head back and laughed out loud. 'It's an ill wind...'

She grinned and pinched the back of his hand. 'When I heard, I thought you'd done it for me.'

'And I would have done in time, darling,' he told her, still laughing. 'But the other way is best—let Stuart earn the favours, not try to buy them with his beautiful cousin.' He bent down and kissed her lips then, and Verity responded by throwing her arms around his neck. They broke off at last and Rupert spoke huskily. 'It's all over now, my dearest love. We are free, and you do love me, don't you?'

'I've never told you, have I?'

'Not in words.'

'Oh, I love you, Rupert. So very, very much. I always have.'

'Have you?'

She wrinkled her nose. 'Well, not at the dinner party or the restaurant. I thought you were pretty grim and moody.'

'You were attracted to me, though,' he persisted hopefully.

She had been, although she had buried it, not wanting to get involved so soon after her other disastrous relationship, but this wasn't the time to thrash that out in her mind—there were other more pressing needs.

She struggled up from the pillows and struggled with the words to tell him. They wouldn't come and her tongue felt swollen and unable to form them. Would he be angry or pleased? He loved her and wanted to marry her, but . . .

'Darling, what's wrong?'

She shook her head and wouldn't look at him. He lifted her chin and her eyes swam as she focused on his face.

'You . . . you said we were free,' she started nervously.

'We are, darling. Once we're married Sarah won't give me any more trouble.'

'It's not that, but . . . but something more. I shouldn't have left you when she told me all those things. I should have trusted you.'

'I understand, treasure. I really do. You were confused and upset and . . .'

She shook her head. 'It was more, Rupert——'

'There's nothing more.'

She had to be honest with him but she was so afraid. 'Rupert, please, please listen to me, and I'll understand if you don't want me.'

'Not want you! I'll always want you.'

She bit her lip and swallowed. 'I ran from El Molino because I loved you so very much and I thought you didn't love me. I was hurting so badly that that was why I was offhand, and I was even cross when you sent the roses without a message——'

'Red roses speak for themselves, Verity,' he told her earnestly. 'So does the moon.'

She nodded vigorously. 'I should have known, but I was so afraid.'

'And you're afraid now, aren't you?'

'Yes,' she whispered and tried to smile, but it wouldn't come. 'And...and I was even more afraid when you asked me to come and live with you because...because something had happened.'

His brow creased and she was even more afraid then, but she hid it because it was no good. She had to tell him, even at the risk of losing him.

'Rupert, when Sarah came to your house——'

'Our house,' he interjected as if to reassure her.

She couldn't repeat 'our house' because it wasn't yet. 'When she told me her child was yours and how you didn't want to know and how you only lived for your work I thought...I thought it would be the same for me, that...that you would reject me too.'

'I decided to work from home for that very reason, Verity. I never wanted the whole commitment with Sarah; if I had I wouldn't have left her alone so much. My love for you is whole and complete, and I want to be with you every minute of the day. It's why I've given you such a hard time over your job. I can't tell you what it meant to me when I called from New York and you said you were giving it up. It's all I've ever wanted. Just the two of us.'

Painfully she widened her violet eyes at him. 'That's just it, Rupert,' she said quietly. 'There isn't going to be just the two of us.'

He smiled. 'The serfs? You'll have to live with——'

'No, Rupert. I didn't mean...' She couldn't finish. She lowered her head and stared at her fingers, entwined in her lap.

There was silence in her tiny bedroom, a deathly silence and then a sound that filled it, every corner of it. Laughter, deep, deep, amazed laughter.

Her head jerked up as Rupert got to his feet and lifted her to him. The room spun and she realised it wasn't the room but her, round and round, clasped in his arms.

'A baby, dear God, a baby!'

The laughter was infectious and when her head stopped spinning she joined him.

'You don't mind?' she cried breathlessly.

'Mind? I'm crazy about the idea.' He held her away from him so that he could drink in her happiness. 'Oh, Verity Brooks Scott, what a clever girl you are. I love you so very much.' His mouth closed over hers and she knew it was going to be all right, and why had she ever doubted it?

She laughed one more time as he lowered her to the bed. 'I thought you didn't like making love in a single bed,' she giggled as she shifted over to make room for him.

'There's always the back seat of my car.'

She linked her arms around his warm neck and pulled him down to her. 'We'll save that for when the baby keeps us awake at night.'

'No baby is going to keep me from what I love doing most in the world,' he rasped as he shifted her robe out of the way, 'making love to my wife.'

'I suppose that means another addition to the staff, namely a nanny,' she teased, and he nipped her ear.

'We'll argue about that at another time,' he told her as his mouth closed over hers, blotting out the very argument that was already forming on her lips.

'Don't be such a baby,' Verity teased as they stepped out into brilliant sunshine in Harley Street.

Rupert slumped back against the railings, holding his arm and looking as if he was going to faint.

'It was only a fingernailful,' she laughed.

He pulled her against him as he supported himself against the railings. 'An armful,' he protested. 'How do you expect me to live and love without my full quota of blood?'

Verity laughed and kissed him on the mouth. 'That arm is already making a full recovery. It's acting as if it doesn't know this is broad daylight and there are hundreds of people milling up and down.'

Rupert glanced up and down the almost deserted street and then slid the arm in question under her coat to slide over her very slightly swollen stomach.

'Happy?' he grinned.

'Ecstatic,' she smiled. 'So we are compatible after all. Your blood is in tune with mine and we're going to have a beautiful healthy baby with violet——'

'Grey eyes,' he finished for her. 'The dominant streak always prevails.'

Those violet eyes twinkled. 'We'll see,' she murmured as she pulled out of his arms and stepped into the back of the car.

'Knightsbridge, Eric,' Verity instructed the chauffeur as Rupert slid in beside her. 'I want a wedding dress that fits before I get too fat,' she whispered in Rupert's ear.

'Then you'll need this to stop the sales assistant's tongue from wagging.' He plunged his hand into his pocket and took out a small, very interesting leather-bound box. He flicked it open, never taking his eyes from Verity's wide violet eyes in case he missed her ecstatic reaction.

'Rupert!' she exclaimed in a rush of excitement. 'Oh, it's... it's totally beautiful.'

'Like you,' he murmured as he took the solitaire diamond ring and slipped it on to the third finger of her left hand. 'It's the perfect twin to the pendant, to seal the promise forever.'

Verity's eyes filled with tears of joy and sparkled brighter than the diamond on her finger. 'So... so this is it. Babies, wedding dresses, engagement rings——'

'Just a minute,' laughed Rupert. 'Where have all these plurals come from? One wedding dress, one engagement ring——'

'One baby?' she murmured, wrapping her arms around his neck and nearly squeezing the life from him in her happiness.

He turned his head and his mouth claimed hers in a deep, deep kiss that promised nothing of the sort. When he finally drew away from her he told her throatily, 'And one official honeymoon.'

'Oh,' Verity uttered, feigning disappointment. 'There was I, thinking life with you would be one long honeymoon.'

'Oh, it will be, and that's another promise, but I did say an *official* honeymoon—you know, the one that generally follows the ceremony, after the champagne and rice throwing——'

'And the cutting up of your tie and auctioning it for our dowry,' she reminded him with a giggle.

'Ah, yes,' he laughed, remembering. 'So that's where you want to go for your honeymoon, is it? El Molino?'

She gazed deep into his eyes, almost afraid that it wouldn't be his choice, but she knew as soon as she saw his grey eyes mist with memories that he wouldn't disagree. They had fought there, and fallen desperately in love there, and their child had been conceived there. It was the only place in the world for a honeymoon.

'Yes,' she whispered dreamily, raising her hand to caress his chin lovingly. 'A honeymoon in Andalucia would be the perfect end to an imperfect affair.'

'And a perfect start to the rest of our lives,' he told her, holding her firmly against him and pressing his warm loving mouth to hers to seal yet another promise.

Next Month's Romances

Each month you can choose from a wide variety of romance with Mills & Boon. Below are the new titles to look out for next month, why not ask either Mills & Boon Reader Service or your Newsagent to reserve you a copy of the titles you want to buy — just tick the titles you would like and either post to Reader Service or take it to any Newsagent and ask them to order your books.

Please save me the following titles:		Please tick √
BREAKING POINT	Emma Darcy	
SUCH DARK MAGIC	Robyn Donald	
AFTER THE BALL	Catherine George	
TWO-TIMING MAN	Roberta Leigh	
HOST OF RICHES	Elizabeth Power	
MASK OF DECEPTION	Sara Wood	
A SOLITARY HEART	Amanda Carpenter	
AFTER THE FIRE	Kay Gregory	
BITTERSWEET YESTERDAYS	Kate Proctor	
YESTERDAY'S PASSION	Catherine O'Connor	
NIGHT OF THE SCORPION	Rosemary Carter	
NO ESCAPING LOVE	Sharon Kendrick	
OUTBACK LEGACY	Elizabeth Duke	
RANSACKED HEART	Jayne Bauling	
STORMY REUNION	Sandra K. Rhoades	
A POINT OF PRIDE	Liz Fielding	

If you would like to order these books in addition to your regular subscription from Mills & Boon Reader Service please send £1.70 per title to: Mills & Boon Reader Service, P.O. Box 236, Croydon, Surrey, CR9 3RU, quote your Subscriber No:..
(If applicable) and complete the name and address details below. Alternatively, these books are available from many local Newsagents including W.H.Smith, J.Menzies, Martins and other paperback stockists from 12th March 1993.

Name:...

Address:..

....Post Code:...........................

To Retailer: If you would like to stock M&B books please contact your regular book/magazine wholesaler for details.

You may be mailed with offers from other reputable companies as a result of this application.
If you would rather not take advantage of these opportunities please tick box ☐

Another Face ...
Another Identity ...
Another Chance ...

The international bestseller
from the author of *Power Play* and
The Hidden Years.

When her teenage love turns to hate, Geraldine Frances vows to even the score. After arranging her own "death", she embarks on a dramatic transformation emerging as *Silver*, a hauntingly beautiful and mysterious woman few men would be able to resist.

With a new face and a new identity, she is now ready to destroy the man responsible for her tragic past.

Silver – a life ruled by one all-consuming passion, is Penny Jordan at her very best.

W●RLDWIDE

4 FREE
Romances
and 2 FREE gifts
just for you!

*You can enjoy all the
heartwarming emotion of true love for FREE!
Discover the heartbreak and the happiness, the emotion and
the tenderness of the modern relationships in
Mills & Boon Romances.*

*We'll send you 4 captivating Romances as a special offer from
Mills & Boon Reader Service, along with the chance to have
6 Romances delivered to your door each month.*

Claim your FREE books and gifts overleaf...

An irresistible offe
from Mills & Boon

Here's a personal invitation from Mills & Boon Reader Service, to become a regular reader of Romances. To welcome you, we'd like you to have 4 books, a CUDDLY TEDDY and a special MYSTERY GIFT absolutely FREE.

Then you could look forward each month to receiving 6 brand new Romances, delivered to your door, postage and packing free! Plus our free Newsletter featuring author news, competitions, special offers and much more.

This invitation comes with no strings attached. You may cancel or suspend your subscription at any time, and still keep your free books and gifts.

It's so easy. Send no money now. Simply fill in the coupon below and post it to -
**Reader Service, FREEPOST,
PO Box 236, Croydon, Surrey CR9 9EL.**

NO STAMP REQUIRED

Free Books Coupon

Yes! Please rush me 4 free Romances and 2 free gifts! Please also reserve me a Reader Service subscription. If I decide to subscribe I can look forward to receiving 6 brand new Romances each month for just £10.20, postage and packing free. If I choose not to subscribe I shall write to you within 10 days - I can keep the books and gifts whatever I decide. I may cancel or suspend my subscription at any time. I am over 18 years of age.

Ms/Mrs/Miss/Mr_____ EP31R

Address_____

_____

Postcode_____Signature_____

Offer expires 31st May 1993. The right is reserved to refuse an application and change the terms of this offer. Readers overseas and in Eire please send for details. Southern Africa write to Book Services International Ltd, P.O. Box 42654, Craighall, Transvaal 2024. You may be mailed with offers from other reputable companies as a result of this application.
If you would prefer not to share in this opportunity, please tick box ☐